C000296557

CAN'T
YOU SEE ME?

Can't You See Me?

CAROL WILLIAMSON

Copyright © 2013 by Carol Williamson.

ISBN: Softcover   978-1-4931-0052-1
               Ebook   978-1-4931-0053-8

All rights reserved. No part of this book may be reproduced or transmitted in any form or by any means, electronic or mechanical, including photocopying, recording, or by any information storage and retrieval system, without permission in writing from the copyright owner.

This book was printed in the United States of America.

Rev. date: 09/23/2013

To order additional copies of this book, contact:
Xlibris LLC
0-800-056-3182
www.xlibrispublishing.co.uk
Orders@xlibrispublishing.co.uk
307255

Dedicated to my four daughters, Kerry, Sheryl, Jennie and Rebekah, because they believed.

CHAPTER 1

Oh no! Here we go again and again! Oh, Rina, let it go, just this once. Leave it. Is it worth the agro? Will I ever accept this—this, I think, disrespect that is shown to us, us being we women. I try not to let my mind start in on this futile journey, this path as well trodden as time itself, maybe, even by the very first woman, the woman who did not listen to honesty but instead listened to the inventor of lies and deceit, the beguiler of women, the betrayer of mankind, and in so doing, brought down pain and regret on all our beautiful heads.

Most assuredly, I will not be the last to tread this uneven road, but as usual, I've taken the first steps before I can stop myself. I firmly argue that it's still a man's world, and the same age-old lament pierces my soul. I know I don't have a job, but I think, in fact I know, that I work just as hard, if not harder than Steve. Steve is my better half or so he likes to earnestly joke. Are we okay as a couple? I like to think we are, but he . . . he thinks I float about the house doing just about nothing all day, which gets right up my nose.

Does it really matter what he thinks if I am secure in the knowledge I am where I want to be in my life? Sometimes, it does matter. He looks on my time spent volunteering at the rape crisis centre as a hobby, so he reasons that, because I don't actually work, I have all the time in the world to look after our home and, more importantly, be a slave to him. I call it slavery; he calls it women's work! I know he is jealous of the time I spend at the centre, but until I get another job, the centre keeps me occupied, and I feel I am actually doing something worthwhile. I will rephrase that — I know I am doing something worthwhile.

My life has been such a cruise compared to that of the women we see each night. Some of the young girls who call with us break my heart. They come in battered, bruised, and terribly frightened. Sometimes, it is the hidden battering and bruising that destroys them and threatens their future lives, and I know we provide the one place where they feel safe and are not judged.

Nearly every night, we get a visit from one of our 'girls' or even one of the mothers, mothers who feel that they, in some way, have caused this — this calamity that has befallen their daughters — or mothers who find they have not the strengths or resources to comfort these damaged children. So they come just to talk, talk to strangers who want to help, and we encourage them to come to us for any solace that we can give. I have sat many nights holding the hands of some distraught mother as her young daughter tells the police over and over again just how violated they were. I have cried with all of them and am not ashamed of one tear. I would do anything to take the hurt away, but in this world, the hurts keep coming.

All I can do for them, apart from the tea and coffee, is to be there and show that someone does care. I also enjoy the company of the other volunteers. They have become my close friends, and I know I sometimes feel closer to my colleagues than to my old friends and even, at times, my own family. This saddens me, and I know I need to do something about this. I admire my colleagues so much for their unstinting compassion that they bring to damaged lives; everyone needs someone to talk to when their backs are against the wall.

My mind is back on my perceived injustices. Can no one else put the milk bottles out? This really irritates me and makes my blood boil. You would think I am the only one who lives here and drinks milk. In actual fact, I don't drink milk, so I threaten to cancel the milkman and making them buy milk from the shop, but Tom, ah Tom, he does not like milk out of a carton, so the milk bottles and who washes and leaves them out stays as a bone of contention between us, among a few other domestic issues that I could mention.

Why, oh why can they not put their clothes in the laundry basket? It is not rocket science as the saying goes. Take your clothes off in the bathroom, then instead of dropping them on the floor, to lie there until I pick them up, just calmly lift the lid of the laundry basket, insert dirty clothes, and put back the lid, and harmony will descend on our home.

If you must drink or eat in the lounge, then when you have finished, please, if you value your mother's life, go into the kitchen, not forgetting the glass, plate, or cup, open the dishwasher that is beside the back door, and place your article inside in the correct position so that it does not have to be washed twice, saving the planet's resources. Do not, in any circumstances, say, for example, 'Phone was ringing', 'Needed the loo', or the best, 'I meant to put it in later'. *Later!* Can someone please explain where or when this 'later' arrives? Because I have waited, oh, so patiently for it, but it never arrives!

If you do not know this, I am now pointing it out to you, for future reference, the floor does not wash itself. I go out to the garage, and I carry the very heavy bucket and cumbersome mop into the kitchen. I struggle to fill the very heavy bucket with water from the tap, and I add detergent and some bleach, which would be harmful to my skin if I splashed myself. I plunge the mop up and down in the soapy water and then I have to put extreme pressure on my arm muscles to squeeze out excess water so that I do not flood the kitchen. Then I have a fifteen-minute workout as I pull and push the mop up and down the floor. If the floor is really dirty, then my workout could be thirty minutes.

Now, you know why your exhausted mother loses her mind when thoughtless people walk with dirty shoes over this clean floor, give it a few hours and the ensuing earthquake will not register 9, give it a few days, even one, and mother will be reasonable. *Just take your bloody shoes off, will you!*

I smile to myself at this range of thinking. Then there comes a memory of Steve dropping his shirt on the floor, a clean shirt that he just did not like the look of on his body. A perfectly good, clean shirt that had taken me ten minutes to iron! If I did not pick this shirt up at once, then it would have to be ironed all over again. Ten minutes, ten minutes, and how many ten minutes would my life be made up of? When I am dying, will I remember all the ten minutes I have spent ironing Steve's shirts.

When did my housework become a thorn in my flesh? It was not so very long ago that I delighted in ironing Steve's shirts; my glory was watching my youthful husband marching forth to earn our daily bread in his pristine armour of shirt and tie. When had the pride gone? Probably after picking up thousands of shirts off the bedroom floor. When did I cease to care how well Steve looked in work? The first time I saw the results of domestic violence; perfectly white, ironed shirts were immaterial! Most men wore them, the good, the bad, and the positively ugly.

CHAPTER 2

That bloody cat, I nearly broke my neck falling over her. I wish she would give her cat affections to Steve and follow him about the way she follows me. Poor cat, Lucy's cat, but because I feed you, you think you are my cat and you give me your cat love. I hope I did not wake anybody up because I'm just moaning for the sake of moaning. I actually love this time of the night by myself, able to do whatever I like, watch TV without someone changing channels, or worse, space hopping from channel to channel, my pet hate, which drives me to near violence, the banality of it. Is this a man thing? I can blissfully read, book after book, without someone calling 'Mum'. I am ashamed feeling like this when I think back to my delight the first time I heard my babies call 'Mum' but a million 'mums' later, the thrill starts to wear thin.

I even sneak out for a jog, something that I know is foolish, but, oh, how I am addicted to the streets when they are empty and the air seems still, quiet, and so soft that it caresses and soothes my bones and calms my mind. For some reason, the night always feels warmer to me than the days, and I find I can relax more and I call it 'my time'. My shoulders loosen, my mind stills, and my heart lifts.

Where do you go, Cat, in your time? Are you chasing vermin, do you know where they hide, or do you wander aimlessly until you accidentally fall over one? During the daytime when you sleep as if you are dead, do you really watch and listen to hear where your victims hide? So when you wake, you know exactly where to search. Oh, you are a clever one! You could teach us all how to manage our days, watch, listen, and then collect, without using too much energy.

Are you seeking a mate? Pick carefully; pick another cat that likes to wander the dark streets at night with you. I envy you, your freedom to roam, and I wish I could run about in the dark as easily as you do, without the fear of being attacked, or do you fear the dark? No. Why would you when you can see better in the dark, see the shapes that frighten me. Goodnight my faithful feline friend. I really do love you. I will see you in the morning when you appear looking for food, your adventures clinging to your cold fur, secrets of the night.

What a lovely calm night! How peaceful and quiet it is! I feel as if I am the only person awake in the whole world, and if I stand very still and don't breathe, I imagine I can hear the stillness. Everything is so different. At night-time, shapes are different. I squint to try and recognise the shapes before me. This is a fantasy of mine when I imagine these every-day shapes as something else. The trampoline in one neighbour's garden is really a castle, Miriam's huge four-by-four is a carriage from ages past, and best of all, Jimmy's gnomes are little people looking for their pot of gold, while Wanda's tiny robin looks down on them from his perch on the bird table, which is really a swimming pool for the fairies.

I hug myself with the sheer joy of living. All my gripes are forgotten as calm settles on my shoulders and happiness fizzles up in my heart, and I turn and look into my home. I look with eyes of a stranger, and I smile at my lovely, warm, and welcoming hallway. I have done a good job in making a comfortable home for my family, and as I stand in the beauty of the starlit night, I am so thankful for my lot in this life. My beloved family are safe in their beds, beds that I know deep down I do not begrudge making everyday of my life, for do they not hold my most precious possessions? My family, I would not change them. Well, only sometimes. I laugh out loud, and turning, I gaze at my neighbour's homes, all shut up and their windows dark.

I imagine their occupants sleeping soundly, some snoring, some dreaming, and others loving, oblivious to the beauty of the night sky, and its treasure of countless stars. I can't recognise the constellations, but I wonder how many stars I can count. But where do I start? They seem to prance and dance before my eyes, and my eyes start to water as I try to focus on just one of these luminous, ageless dots.

CHAPTER 3

Why is it so dark? Where are the stars? Why can I not move? Where am I? What . . . what . . . what has happened? What has happened to me? Maybe if I ask again and again, someone will answer me and then I realise I have not spoken. I can't. Why? There is something over my mouth, that's why, and I cannot even part my lips. What is over my mouth? I try and try to move my lips, but it is futile. What has happened to me? Am I dreaming? If so, I sincerely hope I waken soon. I can't move my head, so I must be dead. Don't be so ridiculous. I must have died in my sleep, but I did not go to bed. I was standing on the garden path, looking at the stars. Was I? Or did I dream it? I am dead, but how? It must have been a heart attack, and it was so quick that I was dead before I hit the ground.

What day is it? Think, think! This is explainable. It is Tuesday, and I was looking at the stars, nothing. Think! It was Tuesday, and I was looking up at the stars. Think! It was Tuesday, and I was looking at the stars, nothing. Where is nothing? I'm not dead, I can open my eyes but I cannot see. Why, why, why, I don't know. I can blink, lots of times, and nothing touches my eyelashes, but all I see is black, dark terrorising black nothing. I can't help it, but oh my lord, I wonder, am I buried already or am I lying in my coffin, waiting to be buried? This is a nightmare. I am dreaming. I must wake up. I can't. I must. I can't. Why can't I? Why can't I? I just can't.

This is ridiculous. I can and will waken. Am I really dead? Am I really dead? I can't be. I won't be. This can't be happening to me. There is some explanation, some simple explanation. Words fail me. What, what, what is licking at my consciousness? No, go away, I don't want to think. I won't think, but my mind is beyond my bidding.

What if my family cremates me? Will I feel the scorching flames lick my flesh, because I can feel? I feel whatever is stuck over my mouth. I feel my eyelashes brush softly over my cheeks. Just stop this right now. This is explainable. I was looking at the stars. It was Tuesday. I spoke to the cat. I was looking at the stars. I was *looking at the stars*.

I am terrified, so terrified I feel physically sick, but I am not terrified enough, because I realise that if I throw up, I will choke and die. How stupid when I am dead already. I am not dead. I can't be dead. It was Tuesday, and I was looking at the stars. Where are the stars? Why is it so thickly dark?

I must be dead. Am I about to find out if heaven exists? I don't want to know, not yet. I want to live. I must try to be calm, but my mind throws a memory that catches me full in the stomach, an article about a woman buried alive, and I know my family, or someone, has made a terrible mistake. They think I am dead, and I'm not. I scream: I am not dead. I am alive. Help me. But because my mouth is covered, no sound comes out, but the scream reverberates around inside my head, making it ache and throb, in waves of pain.

There is a huge malignant tumour of fear growing in my stomach, making it knot and cramp, and I start to cry. I am shuddering, and I feel the huge, hot tears course down my face, and I feel them run down, down my neck, soaking my hair until I am drowning in a pool of salty despair. I can't be dead. If I am dead, why can I feel my tears at all? My tumour of fear grows and grows until it becomes a red sun burning my mind. It explodes, and I drown in the puss and poison. For a while, a white mist envelops me, and I shake and tremor. My mind is a blank, void of reason.

The mist in my mind lifts, and I start to think rationally again. I reason with myself that if I am dead and in a coffin, I would be dressed in a shroud. I would be lying in a soft and silky padded box, but I am lying on something hard and rigid, which is painful to my flesh.

Why can't I move? I try to so hard but I can't. I am paralyzed. Did the roof fall on me? Ah, that's what happened! I knew our roof needed to be replaced. I told Steve it was dangerous. I'll kill him. I'm not paralyzed. How do I know? I can wiggle my fingers and my toes, and is it a joy? No, but it tells me I am not paralyzed. I know I am not, but what is wrong? Yes, I am in an MRI scan. That is why I cannot move. Happy days it will soon be over. I try to remember how long these scans can take. About half an hour I reckon, so I start to count: One, two, three . . . fifteen . . .

CHAPTER 4

What? How long? Where was I? Forty, Fifty! Oh, dear Lord, where was I? My mind struggles and strives to remember; it is so vitally important to know where I was. I will start again, and then comes realisation as I know I have been asleep and I know I am not in a scan, any scan, but where am I? Someone help me. I am going insane. I struggle and struggle and only succeed in hurting my flesh. It is hopeless. I cannot move anything except my hands and feet. Have they sewed my mouth together? No, it is definitely tape that covers my mouth. It pulls at my skin on my face.

I feel whatever it is I am lying on. My fingers touch metal, hard, smooth, unforgiving metal. Oh, now I know, and cold horror fills my mind. What if I am in the mortuary, lying on a mortician's marble table, or worse, maybe the reason why it is so dark is because I am in the morgue's fridge, and they think I am dead? But I am warm, so I can't be in a fridge, and I can smell newness. I smell new furnishings.

I am really terrorising myself with these thoughts, but I can't help myself thinking of the worst-case scenarios, but then hope rises in me, and I am suddenly elated. My body thrills with the hope that when the undertakers come for my body, they will see that I am still warm and blood is still running through my veins, warm, life-giving blood full of oxygen. Then they will rescue me and take me home. What a shock they will get and how cross I will be with everyone, cross but relieved that I am found alive!

Jubilation fills my heart, but just as fast comes a flow of thoughts: What will I do if they really don't notice I am alive? What if I can't move and they start to cut me open? Oh please, someone look at me, feel me, I am alive. Please, please look at me, I am not dead, I am alive!

Will I have to witness my own slaughter, see the knife that will slice through my skin, slice down through layers of skin, fat, muscles, blood vessels into my very core, and will I gaze on the bloody parts of my body that I should never see?

Blood, my life-giving red blood! Will I see it flow like a river, the colour of the deepest sunset when the pathologists make the first cut with their saw? Will they be shocked? Will they be able to stop my river of blood, or will my blood end up in a puddle, a huge puddle on their floor? When my heart stops and all my blood is splashed over walls, doors, floor, will they hose my blood down the drain and will I cease to exist?

My liver, heart, ropes of intestines that can never be put back, they will be damaged by hands that think they are dealing with a dead person. Do they drain off one's blood before they cut, or if I am not to have an autopsy, will I feel the deadening liquid? What is the liquid that they embalm people with? No, not people, corpses. I am not dead! I am alive. I can feel. Oh, somebody, help me! Can't you? Why?

I have to stop these thoughts. I have to because the tumour inside me is growing again and turning into a monster with tentacles that are swinging in all directions and it is eating my insides away with teeth as sharp as razors. How could this happen, in this day and age? Think, think, I tell myself. Think of good, happy times and think of the story you will tell everyone of how the doctors made a mistake, a big, huge, stupid mistake and they thought you were dead. Ha! Ha! Imagine they thought I was dead! I nearly succeed in calming myself when, suddenly, I remember another article I had read. I tried not to let this knowledge into my mind, but it exploded into my thoughts, concerning a woman trapped in a building for ten days after an earthquake. We don't get earthquakes in Knightsbridge Village. I know it was a gas explosion, except we don't have gas.

What happened to me? Please someone help me? Oh no, what of my family? Horror as I think of my family in the same situation as me. Are they near me, can they see, can they hear, or have they tape across their mouths as well? Do they think we are all dead? I can deal with this, but my family trapped, in the dark, lonely, and full of fear, that I could not stand. I am heartbroken with the thoughts of my family feeling as I do at this moment.

Fresh tears pour out of my blinded eyes, enough tears to drown a nation, and I pray that they are not in the same situation as me. The thought of my family, sweet Tom, dizzy Lucy, and my Steve in pain distresses me so much that my chest hurts and I struggle to breathe. My throat is full of tears, and I struggle to swallow them. I need to blow my nose, so simple a thing, but I am prevented from doing normal things. Please, God, look after my family and let them be alive. If someone has to die, let it be me, but save my son, daughter, and my husband. Please do not let harm come to them.

These thoughts of my family bring even more hot, scalding tears that nearly choke me. The faces of my family move in and out of focus in front of my eyes. Tom, my lovely son, he smiles at me, and I am done for. I fall into a dark abbess where I am numbed with shock and fear.

CHAPTER 5

Light! Am I dead, because the light is so intense it pierces my eyes and hurts . . . hurts so much? I cannot see anything except this fierce white glow. Maybe, this is heaven. I squint and screw up my eyes, but still the bright white light fills my vision. I am dead after all and sighing. I feel some sort of relief, warm and welcoming, and I could be happy with this death. At least, I now know I am dead, but deep down, I know I am wrong and I am not dead because I can still feel. I can move my hands and feet. I feel something covering my mouth. What is over my mouth and why am I prevented from speaking?

Have they sewed my lips together? I open my eyes as wide as I can bear because I need them to see that I am very much alive. I must bring attention to myself. See, I am alive, see, I can see, I am not dead. Look, I am wiggling my fingers. Can't you see my feet are moving, can't you see! Look at me, can't you see I am alive! Don't you cut me, don't you dare cut me. I am alive!

No, please no! As my eyes slowly become accustomed to the light, I wish I were dead and safe in heaven. There is no evil in heaven, but there is unfathomable evil in the piercing blue eyes that are looking intently at me. Blue . . . blue eyes that should be beautiful and reflect the world, reflect the sky full of birds, reflect the sea's splendour. No, none of these. These blue eyes that are laughing at me, should really be black, tar black, because they are as dark and evil as hell. Blue eyes staring at me from a face that is no different from most men's faces, but the look from the eyes and the curl of the red lips let me know that here is a man apart from the human race.

Now, I know with a dreadful clarity as to what has happened to me. It is as clear as crystal, and a fearsome terror enters my heart, invading my very soul. I have been taken. Me, Rina, taken . . . taken where?

I look upon the face of this man standing over me. He smiles a smile that holds more menace than a frown, and I feel myself die inside. I am in a room, a bedroom I think. I can see mirrors everywhere, and soon, I see a sight, a horrible sight, a sight that fills my heart with lead. My God, is that me I see, me I am looking at?

It is me! I recognise my hair, my face, my body, my legs, and my feet. I am strapped to some sort of contraption, and now, I notice I am naked. Oh no, now I wish I was dead. I am embarrassed, I want to cover my body, I can't cover myself, I can't move, and my eyes close because I refuse to look on my nakedness. Where am I? I am terrified, and what can I do? Pray—pray that my family or the police rescue me soon? All I can do is look, and as he moves the contraption upright, I involuntarily open my eyes as he places me in front of a full-length mirror. The face looking back at me is so distorted with fear and horror. I don't want to see it, and I quickly close my eyes once more.

Chapter 6

He slaps me hard across my face, and I taste blood, metallic on my tongue. I cringe at the feel of his flesh touching mine. How dare he! 'We can do this the hard way or we can do this the easy way, it is your decision, my dear, but I say you watch,' he snarls at me. I listen to the words he utters. His voice is normal, the tone completely normal, but unfortunately, his voice is full of hate. I can feel it vibrate around us. I feel it lick my skin, washing over my body in waves of menace and horror. He slaps me once more, and even though I don't want to look, I never want to ever again, I dread to look. My instinct for survival makes me open my eyes because I fear that if he hits me again, there is a real chance I might choke, choke on my own blood as my mouth is already too full of blood.

I don't want to die in this room in front of this stinking man. I want to be rescued. What is it I remember that I have to do to stay alive? What did I tell the girls in the centre. What centre? It is so long ago. What day is this? Years seem to have vanished, yet if I concentrate, I might see the stars again. It could be Tuesday, it could be, couldn't it? If it is still Tuesday, this would all be a dream, and I would never roam the empty streets again, but I wasn't roaming the streets . . . I didn't go out, did I? I don't remember.

I slowly open my eyes. I want to close them right away, and I have to call on all my strength and determination to keep them open because I hate what I see. Oh, how I hate what I see! I see an amazing contraption made of some sort of metal; it reminds me of the trolley Hannibal Lector was strapped to in the movie *Silence of the Lambs*. Hannibal was evil; he needed to be constrained. I am not bad, so why am I strapped to this thing?

I am very tightly strapped with large brown leather straps, to this thing. I cannot move a muscle, but the worse part about it is I am completely naked. Where are my clothes, my jogging suit? How did he manage to remove my clothes without me knowing? Did he remove my clothes or did someone else, two or more of them? No, please, my fevered mind could not deal with others. He is bad enough, more than bad enough. He has me terrified.

These stupid, stupid questions that jump and flit about in my mind, they are destroying my concentration. I need to stay sharp. I need to focus so that I can try to escape. 'Escape? Who am I trying to kid!' It is hopeless. I am at his mercy. No, I refuse to give up hope. There will be a way, but I need to keep calm. He will make a mistake. Keep calm and then take the chance, so I need to focus.

I look at this man before me, and I study him. Isn't this what you are supposed to do, remember everything about your assailant? But he is naked, just like me. I'm going to be sick. I do not want to see his nakedness, but I know I have to memorise him so that I can help the police find him when I am free. I look everywhere but down. I refuse to look at his private parts; the thought of them has me repulsed.

He is average, average, an average man with average length, average colour hair. He is an average man that exists in every street, a man that will never stand out from the crowd, but he is a chameleon. His very averageness hides his difference; it hides his evil. Oh, how I wish his evil was hidden from me!

I am spreadeagled, and I blush to see my breasts hanging free and my vagina exposed! How unlovely the human body is in cold blood! A naked body over sixteen-years-old needs soft lighting; it needs passion and love to show its beauty. This cold-blooded showing of his and my nakedness is just plain ugly; there is no love to clothe it in splendour.

He laughs to see the crimson stain creep over my face as he roughly clasps one of my breasts in his hand. I notice that his hands are soft and his nails are clean and well manicured, and I am disgusted with myself for even noticing this. It is then that I notice with mounting horror the unfamiliar marks on my body, bruises dark and ominous, cuts deep and scurrilous, and teeth marks, lots of them. Heaven, help me! I am so horror-struck I forget to breathe, and when my fevered mind cools, I struggle to sniff enough air through my nose. My head reels with lack of oxygen. I try to strain against this contraption to no avail; I cannot move.

He has bitten me; the bites are deep, and blood trickles from a few, so how do I not remember the pain? I realise he must have drugged me for how could I not have felt the pain and I did not feel the pain of these inflictions. I begin to wonder just how long I have been here. Hope flares up in me. Surely someone has noticed I am missing; surely, he could not have taken me far.

A car! Oh no, could he have bundled me into a car? If so, I could be anywhere, and who will find me now? My flame of hope that someone is searching for me flickers and dies, hope is extinguished, hope of rescue is snuffed out, and my hope now is that he drugs me again, my hope is he gives me too much and I never waken up to this horror again.

My God, where am I, why has no one come to find me? Why, why, why me? What have I ever done to deserve this torture? I did not put myself in danger. Yes, you did, I tell myself; you ran about the night streets at ungodly hours, you would not listen to others' advice. No, Rina knew better, Rina thought things like this happened to other people, tragedy did not come knocking on Rina's door.

When I read stories of abductions, I used to rant and rave that I would never be grabbed easily. I would scream, bite, yell, kick, and be dragged screeching, but I would not go quietly, which I secretly thought some victims did. Here is the bold Rina, taken without a sound, taken so quietly and professionally that she did not even see the danger coming. Now, I walk in their shoes. Now, I understand, only too clearly do I now understand.

Hot tears of self-pity run down my face and splash on my naked breasts. They flow down to my feet and form a puddle that I wish could grow and grow and flood this room so that I might drown in their salty depths. I cannot stand this. How can I cope with this abuse? Can I cope with it? I am choking on my sobs, sobs of despair and hopelessness.

CHAPTER 7

How am I to live, live with this dirt, filth, when every part of my being longs for oblivion? How to live when I really would prefer to die? If he gave me the chance to kill myself now, I would take it. Ah, Rina, would you really? I might, rather than stay here with my tormentor, this disgusting excuse of a man, this demon disguised as a man.

Once again, I earnestly pray for death to take me as I watch this monster play with me. Play, it is a good description of what he does with me, and the pain is so unbearable but is bearable because I bear it, my body does, and it doesn't die, but I understand now about there being a worse death than a physical one. Oh, I do understand. I am curled up and dying inside, and I am so lonely in my heart. I am alone in the presence of a devil.

I am crying again, and I know he likes me crying by the smirk on his disgusting face. I know this is all about power, and that is why he has me strapped up so tightly. He likes me to know that he can do whatever he wants to do to me and there is absolutely nothing I can do about it. I am at his mercy, but mercy is one thing I will never receive from this cruel man, who delights in my cries of agony.

I stare at this 'man', whom I faintly recognise, and I wonder if he is one of the men whose wife visited the crisis centre. Have I angered him in some way and so much that he is taking his revenge out on me in such a brutal way? Am I to pay for helping some woman? Am I to pay dearly for my love? My colleagues warned me about retaliation. They warned me to be aware of some of the perpetrators, but I thought I was immune to danger: It would never happen to me, could it? These things happened to other people, not to me, Rina, and just who do I think Rina is or rather was?

When he looks at me, the hairs stand up at the back of my neck, and I know I am in the presence of a monster. Evil has come knocking at my door, and I am one of the 'other people' now. I try to connect with him by making my eyes soft and pleading, but he just looks at me with eyes as pale as death itself, eyes that have no soul, just wickedness so deep they petrify my being.

How will I reach this 'human being', how can I touch him, how can I make him see I am human and I am a wife, a mother, my family love me, I am important to lots of people, I am not some one who will not be missed, I am not a nobody? How? My tears have no effect; it is as if they are invisible. I am in trouble, deep fathomless trouble.

` I feel shame; my face and body are blazing with hot strong shame. Shards of pain pierce my head, my heart is thumping, and I sob and shudder, my breaths short and painful. Why am I ashamed? It is certainly not my fault that I needed the toilet and I have wet myself. I feel the warm wet urine splash against my cold legs and bare feet. I urinate for what seems like hours to me; on and on, it flows like a steaming stream. I try to stop, but the pain is awful and how he laughs, oh, how cruelly he laughs, then he forces something inside me so violently that the urine clinging to my legs is soon tinged pink with my blood.

Once again, I scream in my head, and thankfully, I pass out to blessed oblivion, but I am not to enjoy this oblivion. No, oh no, I rapidly come to. I am in a large shower, and he is hosing me with freezing cold water, slicing my skin, each pinprick of water like a lance piercing my body. I am still on the contraption as he hoses me down, and even though I am in so much wracking pain and my mind in a tumbling turmoil, I actually register how ingenious this contraption is, and I know with a dreadful certainty I will not be able to break free from it.

How deep can my heart fall, how big can my terror grow, how strong can my mind be to cope with this nightmare that I find myself in? How can I survive this onslaught of violence against my flesh? How long before he goes too far in his 'games' and he kills me? I, unfortunately, will soon find the answer to this question.

CHAPTER 8

'We are awake again and nice and clean. I like it with a cold woman. I don't like sex warm. I like it cold like death,' he says as he wheels me out of the bathroom, and the play begins again, and again and again until . . . until he has had enough, or rather enough for the moment. How will I suffer more of this? If I could scream out loud, I imagine that would help me with the pain, but the screaming I do in my head is like a vice that tightens with every onslaught of abuse.

I pray for death to take me and bring me oblivion, and I wonder just how long I can live with this abuse before I really begin to lose my mind. Losing my mind would be a blessing, a mixed blessing, to leave this bodily pain behind and float above my consciousness. How sweet! But I can't allow this to happen. Why not switch off, because I still harbour a slight hope that someone will rescue me?

It is a tiny, slight hope that flickers deep down in my soul. It is still alight, it may be weak, but nevertheless, it burns within me. So I pray. I pray I will be rescued, will be rescued soon, surely someone will come for me.

I cannot move, but I writhe and writhe, shudder, and shake as each nerve ending cries out at the horrors inflicted on my unwilling body. What gives someone the right, why does he think he has the right to do this to me? Has he no compassion, no mercy? How can he do this and do it with such enthusiasm? He does it because he can, and I am repulsed and sickened. My mind is reeling, and my heart is sore, but still he goes on and on in his determination to sadistically rob me of life and decency. Is my destruction his fulfilment, my pain his pleasure, my tears his happiness, or my heartache his joy? What is going to happen to me? My little flame flickers and dulls. No, I refuse to let whatever hope I have be extinguished.

CHAPTER 9

Dark like an ominous presence envelops me, and I am back in the place where I was before the light. How I prayed for light! How I earnestly wanted some light! But now, I welcome this blackness like a loved old coat. I seek the comfort of familiar warm cloth. Allow me to stay here. I feel safe here. Right now, my hope is dying, and I don't care. How can I live with the memory of what he did to me?

How? I reason, can I live my life normally again after this degradation to my body and soul? How do I face my children with the knowledge of these horrors all over me? Will I ever wipe this nightmare from my mind? I am forever changed; this brute has changed me forever. Only if I let him, but how can I possibly stop him from obliterating me from Rina? Rina is gone, never to return.

My husband, I know he and I will never have the easygoing lovemaking that we have enjoyed in our marriage ever again. He will never want to touch me after this. This vile creature has branded me with the tattoo of his vicious lust; he has branded me his, never to be touched by another. Are this rapist's hands the last hands that will ever touch me? Surely not! This is not my fault. Why should I be punished?

Visions of my husband and I making love drift across my consciousness: our lovely bed, Steve and I lying entwined together, naked, beautiful, oh how beautiful, so beautiful compared to this lust and perversion! How different is this deviant sex that this horrendous jailer inflicts on my body compared to my lovemaking with Steve?

Steve and I have experimented with sex; we have used toys, but they were all used to pleasure both of us, pleasure us in love. I loved to pleasure my husband, but it was love we shared, not this sexual abuse. There is certainly no love and the pleasure; it is all this jailer's and his alone. Will I want to make love to my husband ever again? Will I ever recover enough to want my husband again? Will he want me?

I can almost feel Steve's touch on my flesh. I concentrate, and I can feel his hands as they gently roam over my skin, bringing healing to my wounds. My body calms as I imagine Steve's body and soft familiar hands. I know his touch, his strong, gentle fingers that bring me to exquisite climax. He is stroking my breasts, soft tender strokes as fine as gossamer and as smooth as silk. Oh, Steve, you are here with me in my dreams. This is working for me. I feel you and I smile as I relinquish myself to the feeling of peace as my dream engulfs me. I am floating above my agony, imagining myself at home. This is lovely, and this is a weapon.

I can use this weapon; I will use this weapon. I am not defenceless. When *he* touches me, I will imagine it is Steve. *His* hateful, painful embraces will be replaced with my memories of my husband's lovemaking. I have a weapon now. I have a strong shield, and one day I will have a sword, and then I will put on my armour and do battle with my tormentor. Will my shield save me from his weapons of mass destruction and my sword strike a deadly blow? I am not sure, but I must keep hope alive. I must.

Why am I torturing myself with these mindless thoughts? Why am I picturing myself with Steve? The comparison is making a bad situation worse. Worse! My life has been taken, and I can never bring it back. Never bring it back to what it was. Gone like the wind, gone forever. Rina will never be Rina again.

Oh my God, please let me be found with some particle of myself remaining. Please, dear God, let him leave me here and please let me die soon so that I never have to look on that evil, cunning face again or feel his disgusting hands on my body once more. If I can't die, let my mind shut down for ever. I prefer to be a vegetable to reliving this nightmare over and over again. Please help me. I want to die. I sobbed and sobbed hot salty tears, and I shook and trembled violently until exhausted sleep claimed me and I fell into peace. What price peace?

Chapter 10

'Boy, you are one hot woman. I can feel the heat off you, and you know I don't like warm women. I told you I like my women cold, so you will have to go into the shower. Now why are you crying? Don't you like to be clean? There is no pleasing you, is there? What, what is wrong? Ah, you need the toilet, and I just thought you were happy to see me. While you are in the shower, please go to the toilet because we don't want any accidents, do we?' he sniggers. He is naked; he is always naked. Why? But I am too exhausted with pain to reason it out. I am starting not to care.

Crying? How have I any tears left? Where are they all coming from? I am dragged from the welcome darkness that I had cloaked myself with into the bright white room of my nightmares. No, don't show me the light. I want to stay in my dark warm place where he cannot see me and where I cannot see myself. I don't want to see, but I need the toilet so badly. This is dreadful, awful, and so degrading. He is determined to inflict as much trauma on me as possible.

I always locked the bathroom door when I used the toilet at home. I liked my privacy. But here, I need the toilet so badly, and I don't have a choice, so I let the urine run down my legs, and I defecate where I stand, as my legs and feet are splashed with my own bodily fluids. His cruel laughter rolls around me, and my face fills with a scarlet shame. My nose fills up with the putrid smell of my excrement. God, how ashamed I am!

A hot blast of water burns my tortured flesh, and I smell lavender, and I puzzle at the feeling of pleasure this smell gives me. He showers me for what seems hours, and he studies me inch by inch, his eyes taking in every part of me. I cringe and try to make myself small and disappear. Where could I vanish to, where could I hide, how can I hide?

I am so ashamed because I can't hide my faults from him, and I am furious at myself for caring what he thinks of me. I do care. I care about how my stomach is still flabby from the birth of my two children. I am ashamed of the stretch marks that weave their fine tapestry across my breasts and hips. I know that I would hide them if I could. Why am I even allowing these thoughts to enter my head? This man is not worth my anxious thoughts about my bodily failures, so why am I thinking this? Because I am a woman, that's why, with all the insecurities that airbrushed celebrities gazing out from magazines have foisted on us.

Freezing water makes me start, and his laughter bangs off the glass shower walls, smashes against my bones, and pulsates around this bathroom like a roaring demonic ogre. The freezing water is so sore and so very cold I shake and shiver until the sound of my teeth clenching joins his rabid laughter. My fingers clench, my toes curl, my skin turns red, blue, then purple. Is he trying to freeze me to death, something I had not thought of?

Even though I am absolutely frozen, I still feel his penetrating fiery eyes as they slake my body. What is he looking for? He is looking at his work of art. Does his smile or rather grimace mean he is pleased with what he sees or is he congratulating himself on a job well done? I am left to drip dry, just like I used to do with my husband's shirts.

CHAPTER 11

Once again, I study the bathroom, and I notice it is a wet room, white tiles on floor, ceiling, and walls, white, blinding white that shelters the black evil in its midst. I stare at *him*, and it is almost a delineation that I can see around his body, black on the pristine white. It is the evil that emanates from his soul. What soul? He does not have one. The black line pulsates and throbs, sending waves of evil over the cold air towards me. I try to think of my family, but my shield is too thin, and it is powerless against these evil forces. They pierce my protection, and I am vanquished. I am powerless against this mad man.

I acknowledge it is relatively easy for him to wheel me about in this place. It is a really nice bathroom, very clean as well as very white, but the smell of lavender is so overpowering I start to feel sick to my stomach. My head hurts. My back, my legs, my breasts, I hurt everywhere, but I hurt, most of all, deep in my bleeding heart. A sob chokes my throat. I struggle to swallow, so I cry in my mind 'please', but no one answers my plea.

'Now, you are just as I like you, cold, dry, and delicious, and if you decide to behave and don't go all tense on me, aren't you enjoying yourself? My, my, what else have you to do? Would you rather I ignored you? If you behave, or rather if you give me a really good time, I will have a lovely present for you. You might even see your wonderful family again. Now, wouldn't that be something else? You do realise they have just noticed you are missing. Tut, tut what a delightful family! Come on, what are you crying for? You know you really like it rough. All women do. They pretend to be innocent, but in reality, they are born whores. *My*, you taste gorgeous, and I love the smell of lavender. It does something to me.'

My jailer smiled, a smile of menace, the awful smile of the victor when he claims his reward. The smile worn by men from all nations, for all time, as the battle is won and they are the conquerors. We are the collateral. We women are the prize. We are women, flesh and blood, the other half of you, created for man to love, not hurt. We were made to be a helpmeet for you, a partner and comfort. You were given your superior strength to protect, cherish, and love us; instead, rogue men have wandered off the path of God and descended into hell where they have learned hell's instructions on how to treat women. My conqueror is definitely doing his master's work for him.

What pleasure he got from the abuse he inflicted on my body was beyond my understanding, but pleasure he got, and I fought hard and furious to keep the bile from choking me as I watched, at his command, for he checked at times to make sure I was watching. How I hated to see the look of pure ecstasy that filled his ugly face and his eyes! How they would glaze over like a lizard's but the evil would still blaze through and scald me, making me squirm and retch! I was terrified of being sick. I knew I would drown in my own vomit if I did. My throat was raw with swallowing so often. My eyes red raw from crying, but my body was red raw from torturous inflictions.

I wondered what had happened to make this man so evil, what circumstances had affected him so badly that he became this twisted being, standing before me. I looked but tried not to see, then I tried to rise above my predicament and pretend it was someone else I could see in the mirror, but the agonising pain always brought me back to reality where I saw my frightened self gazing back at me from the myriad of mirrors, me with dark horror-struck eyes flowing with millions of tears.

Was this really happening to me, Rina, the pain as he violently pitched me and the contraption backwards and proceeded to aggressively rape and ravish me? Let me know that yes, this was indeed Rina, helpless Rina, trussed up and vulnerable. I tried, believe me, I really tried hard to imagine that I was in my lovely bed with Steve and we were making love, but it was next to impossible. The pain, the awful body-wrecking pain was so intense that I had to concentrate fully to try and make my mind deal with it. I was caught up in a whorl of pain and anguish that swirled me around and around until I disappeared into a black hole.

Chapter 12

'Eat, eat, you bitch. I hate skinny women, and I have not finished with you yet. You don't get to call time. You don't forget how you are the first I have taken home. The rest I could only enjoy for a few nights until I had to hurriedly get rid of them, and I hate to hurry. It takes the pleasure out of loving. Something is always missing when I hurry, but I can have you for as long as I desire and in the comfort of my own home. You don't know what trouble I went to for you, to make you feel at home. What luxury, but it is only what I deserve. I have been so clever and patient, and patience always pays off.

'Eat, or I will do things to you, pain that you never imagined in your wildest dreams. Pain so exquisite you will feel orgasm over and over, until you want to kill yourself to get release from this torturing pleasure. There I told you, I warned you, you have only yourself to blame. Eat or I will. Ha, ha, so that is your plan. I am not stupid, dear. You think I will kill you, but you are wrong, so very wrong. I won't kill you, but if you make things awkward for me, I will hurt you so much you will die over and over again. Do you know how much abuse the human body can take? I do, for I have experimented with lots of bodies, most more beautiful than yours, dear. Do as you are told, and you will not find out. Although that is, I am afraid, not a promise. Thank you, my dear. Ah, you like my smoothie. Then you can have it every day, and it is in your own interests as it will keep you alive but for just as long as I need or desire you.'

He has broken my wrist. I know it is broken because the pain is really bad so I accept the straw he offers me. It is pink. How appropriate! Pink for cancer. He is worse than cancer. Cancer kills; it does not violate. He has cut a tiny hole in the tape covering my mouth, just large enough for a straw, and I suck a foul-tasting liquid up and into my mouth, and I involuntarily vomit, but he does not move to take the tape off my mouth. Instead, he watches me, with foul interest and a smile on his face. He knows that my instinct to live will be strong, and it is, so I choke and choke and vomit comes down my nose, and tears fill my bulging eyes and I choke and choke until I manage to swallow the vomit back down my throat and I force myself to keep it down. My head is swimming with a lack of oxygen, and everything goes black as I pass out. Peace.

Pain, what awful pain I feel, my wrist hurts. I hurt. Where? Everywhere, and when I can focus on my reflection in the mirror, I know why. I look like I have been in an accident; blood sparkles red on my body. My breasts throb, and I am horrified to see my right nipple hanging off. I am covered in blood, and the pain between my legs is indescribable. Where is he? I need the toilet. My head begins to reel and swirl. The smell is rank. I open my eyes and wish I hadn't. He is right in front of me, staring into my eyes, his eyes bottomless pits of evil.

'So we are alive. What a woman, what a lucky night to find you practically on my doorstep! You were handed to me on a plate, you stupid bitch. What where you doing, looking up in the air? I am sorry I was rough with you, but you asked for it. You pretended to be asleep, and I can't have that. You must enjoy this experience with me. You are my partner, and when I desire you, you will be ready and willing, or else . . . I can't help my reaction if you pretend, so don't. You are disgusting. Come let me wash you in my lavender and then I will give you your surprise, big, huge, a wonderful surprise. I can hardly wait to see your face.'

CHAPTER 13

How can I be thankful to this mad man? But I am. I am pitifully thankful for the warm soothing water he hoses me down with. I accept with gratitude the sweet smelling lavender cascading over my bruised and lacerated body, and once again, I marvel at the construction of this trolley that he can manoeuvre me about on.

'Come, you can dry in the beautiful sunshine that is shining through the window, and you can gaze on your gift that I have kindly bestowed on you. Now, no tears, just enjoy the family scene, and we will have a party later to celebrate the change in our relationship.'

Relationship! I don't want a relationship with this man, but I know that my only hope is trying to make him see me as a person, a real person. How can I reach him if I cannot talk to him? I realise that is one of the reasons why he keeps the tape over my mouth. I vow to make him feel for me and pity me enough to let me go. Deep down, I know this is futile. If this creature can inflict the horrors he has on me, what feeling do I imagine he possesses, what can he ever feel? He has no heart, but without hope, what have I? Despair.

My house, my home, my car, my son, I nearly faint with the shock of being able to see them. Help me, help, help, help me, I scream in my head until I know a migraine is starting, but I can't help myself even though I know my son will not hear me. I still scream. I struggle and flex my body against my contraption, and Elation gives way to despair, but I gaze with an incredible hunger on my son, my Tom. How I wish

I had one of your huge hugs now! He is standing in the side garden, and I can tell he is upset by the way his shoulders are hanging, as if he has lost his shoulder blades. I realise I am being held captive in a room in the house next to our house. The window I am looking out of looks across our garden to our drive, and I can actually see our front door.

I will be found. I can be found. I am practically at home. Just look up, and you will see me, I am here, I am with you. Come for me, come and get me, take me away from this man, and make me better. You must see me; you must feel me near you. Why, why are you waiting, why can't you see me? How hard is it to find someone in the next house? Did you look for me at all? How could you not find me? I am here right next door! For the love of God, just look up!

Steve, oh, my husband, is it really you that is putting your arms around Tom and comforting him. Tom hugs you back. I close my eyes, and I try to feel your two pair of arms hugging me, and I think that if I concentrate really hard, I can make you sense me near you. I open my eyes, and you are looking intently up the street, and I pray, look up, look up, please just look up, you will see me, you must see me. I need you. Why can't you sense I am here at the window looking down on you? If only I could move or if I could throw myself forward so that this contraption would fall against the window? I would not care if I fell out of the window. What injuries would I suffer worse than what I already have suffered in here? Even if I were to die, it would be preferable to this incarceration, but I know I don't want to die. I want to live, and I want to be found and given back to my family. I despair at the thought of my family's pain as they wonder what has happened to me.

A police car pulls up my driveway. It stops, and two policemen step out and shake hands with my husband and my son. Happy days. They are large and substantial, and hope flares in my soul; they are policemen, guardians of us all. I will be rescued now. How reassuring their presence makes me feel! My husband and son lead the two policemen into our home, and I am filled with hope: I will be found. They will find me soon, and when they do, I will beat the life out of this creature. I will hit him so hard so many times that he will be unrecognisable, and I will injure him so badly that he will never be able to do what he has done on me to anyone else. I am elated and laughing in my heart, but he senses this, and I know at once I have made a grave mistake in letting him see a spark of hope in me. He will crush me.

CHAPTER 14

'Nice and dry just in time. I see we have guests. I have had the pleasure of your company for two days, and in all that time, your family did not even notice you gone. You are better off with me. You mean more to me than you do to them because I, I would notice you gone at once. Ha, ha! Now, I need to check that we have everything in order for our visit from our friendly neighbourhood cops. Can't have them finding anything out of order now, can we? Do you see my treadmill, how it leaves marks on the floor just like your pram does? This is my gym, and what do people do after a . . . how shall we put it? A good workout, and you know how hard I work out, don't you. They shower. I shower with lavender oil with a smell so strong that it disguises any other odours. Did you know lavender kills bacteria? I kill women.'

I watch as he removes the bed coverings, gorgeous white bed linen that I would like to own, then he lifts the mattress off the bed, and I watch as he lifts the cover off the bed base, then he lifts the top and side off the base, and I am looking at my dark place. It is so simple, yet so ingenious. I notice that it has a waterproof backing, and I wonder how I can breathe in this small place. He informs me that the bed is made of special breathable material and that he has made thousands of tiny holes all over the mattress. Holes, that unless you were looking, especially for them, they were practically invisible. He injects my arm with something, and I am instantly drowsy. He presses a button on my contraption, and it rises, and he is then able to slot me in to the base of the bed.

I lie looking up at the ceiling, and I notice there is a bulb missing from the three-armed chandelier. He has not thought of everything; this I might be able to use, when I am rescued. I need to memorise everything. No, not everything. He leans in and kisses me on top of the gag covering my mouth, and I imagine I absorb some of his breath through the tiny hole in the tape and I gag. Tears shoot out of my eyes. How he laughs!

'Night, night, my lavender lovely,' he says before he replaces the coverings of the bed. I am back in the dark, and I am frantic. They will never find me in here. I must stay awake. I open and close my eyes, but to no avail. They droop and droop until I know they are closing. I shudder trying to keep awake. I must be awake when they come to rescue me. I must make a noise, and they will hear me. I will make sure they do.

Before I succumb to sleep, I know with a certainty that I am lying in my coffin. One day, when he tires of me, he will leave, and I will be found by some poor unsuspecting person who will have nightmares for the rest of their lives, or this hateful bed will be sent to the dump, and I will be slowly chewed and eaten by rats before I am torn apart by the teeth on the council's crusher. I hope by then, I am dead. I must stay awake. I need to know when my saviours come for me, and not for a minute do I think I might not be found. I need to believe. I sleep.

TOM

Chapter 1

My mum is gone. She has disappeared into thin air, and every day I miss her more. How can someone just disappear? Where are you, Mum? Mum, Mum, Mum, please come home. I promise I . . . we will all be different. I am so sorry for the way I treated you. I will be better, I promise you.

I wish I could go back to Tuesday night because I heard Mum trip over the cat and I was going to call her into my room for a chat, but I fell asleep, and the next morning when I could not find her, I just went on to school. How can we go on doing normal things? Should I not have known that my mum was in trouble and needed me? Why did I not try to find her? Mum carried me inside her for nine months. I am part of her flesh, so why didn't I sense that she was in trouble? How did I not know? Why did I not? Oh, do something, somebody, do something. Nobody seems to know what to do. What has happened to our lives? We are floundering. These sorts of things happen to other people, people who are somehow to blame but not to us. We are normal people.

I knew something was up because she had not washed my rugby kit. I could not remember a time when my mum had not washed my kit and put it back all clean and ironed in my gym bag. As soon as I opened my bag, the smell of my decomposing kit told me Mum had not washed it, so I have no excuse, and I feel I have let her down. Mum always washed my kit, so I should have known. Why didn't I? What is wrong with me? Will I never have her wash my kit again? I will gladly wash my own kit if I can have my mum home. I wanted to go out and search for her, but the police would not let me go. In fact, they would not let any of us leave the house for ages. I argued, and I even physically fought with them, but I believe they thought one of us had a hand in Mum's disappearance and they wanted to observe us closely. Come on, we are normal people. We do not go around hurting people, but I hurt my mum. I did not mean to, but I did.

Every time I left my clothes lying where I had stepped out of them and every time I left my dishes where I had been eating off them, I hurt my mum. I told the police that and then the questions came fast and furious. I hated the questions they asked me. I loved my mum, I wanted her found, and I wanted our family back. Dad told me I was stupid for saying I had hurt mum, and just what did I think I could achieve except to make the police even more suspicious of us all, even he did not understand what I was trying to say. The questions they asked Dad reduced him to tears, and I was angry and felt so sorry for him until I found out why.

When Dad told me about Susan, I thought I would kill him. What a scumbag! How can he be so disgusting, my own father gadding about with a young girl? Susan, how dare she hurt my mum and hurt her so badly that she left us! I could kill her as well as my dad. They are both disgusting. Had Mum found out about her and run away? No, I will never believe that my mum willingly left us. She is not like that. Mum would have beat the life out of Dad and taken him to the cleaners. She would have given it to Susan as well. Mum was frightened of no one and loved us to bits, which worries me more because if she did not run away, then what has happened to her?

Chapter 2

The police think my dad killed Mum. I know they do. They watch him all the time. I believe they are waiting until he slips up and then they will have him. My dad is an adulterer, but I know he is not capable of murder. He is especially not capable of murder and then acting as if nothing had happened. The police give him a hard time, but I am no comfort to him because I know he did not hurt Mum but I hate him for betraying her, so he carries some blame. When my mum comes back, you will be in so much trouble. I would not like to be in your shoes, Susan. Mum will throttle you and send you back to the hole you crawled out of. Don't ever come calling here, if you know what is good for you.

I stay in my room all the time now. Dad thinks I am watching TV, but I am playing over and over in my mind all of our actions, trying to see if there was a sign that I had missed. It is like a loved old movie that is starting to disintegrate. I try to cherish it, I take it out most days, especially nights, and I polish it, but in trying to preserve it, I am destroying it, and in the process, I am destroying myself. But I am incapable of stopping. I am consumed by thoughts of how we failed our mum.

I never noticed Mum upset or ever crying. She complained about us not helping around the house, but she did it half-heartedly, and she got on with it. Was she just fed up? Had she had enough? She told me every day how much she loved me and how important I was to her, and with a pain in my heart, I could not remember ever telling Mum I loved her, and now it might be too late. Too, too late to tell Mum I love her. It can't be, or I will die. I can't think like this, for if I do, then I am acknowledging that Mum is gone forever. The thought of never seeing her again brings me to my knees, and I earnestly pray to God to help me find my mum. We must find her; I hope the police find her soon. I hope they find her alive. I can't allow my mind to dwell on the possibility that she is dead, no way. I would know, I would, then, I think, just the way you knew she was gone. My stupid sister spends all day crying or texting her friends. I can't talk to her, and we are falling apart as a family. I don't want to talk to Dad or Lucy. I am starting to hate them.

CHAPTER 3

We have a really nice policewoman living with us called Sharon, and she tries her best to talk to us, but she resembles my mum, and every morning when I first see her, I am shocked and then furious when I realise that Sharon is not Mum come home. She is puzzled by my treatment of her, but I can't explain it to her. She makes all our meals, and another policeman brings our groceries to the back door. The meals are quite all right, but I find I can't eat much before I start to feel sick to the stomach at the situation we are in. Mum, where are you?

We are not allowed to speak to the newspapers, as if we would wish to. I won't even speak to my friends, and before long, they get the message and they stop calling. I am floundering in a sea of bewilderment. Where, oh where is my mum? Why can't they find her?

I don't believe they are really trying; they seem to have forgotten that they ever thought Dad was involved in her disappearance. They are treating him as if he was the victim. Him, the victim? I don't think so, but he will be when my mum finds out about Susan. Is that not why she ran away? If not, a white mist fills my thoughts for I will not go where I might have to acknowledge that Mum will not be back. Something hangs in the periphery of my mind that threatens to tear me to shreds, so I push it away, down into a dark place where I will one day have to visit but not yet. Please, God, not yet, while I have some hope. Hope, every time I leave the house and return, hope flares in my heart that this will be the time I will find Mum home.

Every time I walk down our familiar but now alien street filled with neighbours who stare at us in silent accusation, I let my heart fill with hope, but hope is once again vanquished, and my mum is still missing. Will this be the story of my life? Will this sad story ever have an ending? I write my preferred ending each day in my mind. This has to have a happy ending or . . . or what? What else is there to live for?

CHAPTER 4

I woke up this morning, and I accepted that I might never see my mum again, and I think that the police feel the same way because they have told us we can go out and about again. Why, why mum is still missing? Please don't give up. I can't because if I do, I will cease to exist.

It was my fault; I feel it and deep down know it. I could have prevented it, but I didn't, and now I have to somehow find a way of living with my guilt.

Our friendly policewoman has gone, but we are still well fed by our new neighbour. Ricky moved in next door to us a few months ago, and I'm sure he wonders what sort of neighbourhood he has moved into with mothers disappearing into thin air. He is really friendly, and I find I can talk to him. He knows when I am having a bad day, and we go for a walk, and he lets me run on and on about my lovely mum and how much I miss her. He is the only one I tell how I cry myself to sleep at night and how I skip school a lot of days and I wander around town hoping that I will see her.

I have placed adverts in all the newspapers begging Mum to come home and telling her how much I miss her. Ricky encourages me in these pursuits. He has all the time in the world for me compared to my dad, who, I know, is off sleeping with his whore, and as for my sister, she has a boy friend whom she stays with most weekends. He seems to have replaced Mum in Lucy's life. Have they forgotten Mum already?

Dad made an appeal on TV asking for Mum to come home or if anyone had information to get in touch with the police. I think he is secretly pleased that Mum is gone although I would like to think that he hopes nothing bad has happened to her.

I did not know. How could I know they were such amazing actors, that my family was one big sham? Did my mum have a lover as well as my dad? Were we all just living a big fat lie? I hope she is well, and I hope she is happy. I just wish she would let me know, for then I might be able to live without the guilt and the fear, fear of never knowing what could have happened. I need to know, the very air that I breathe needs to know so that I can live.

I pray that if she was murdered, she did not suffer. Murdered! Oh my God, how can I even utter this thought, never mind think it. I try not to dwell on the horror movies I have watched and the dreadful scenes I have gorged my eyes on, and I pray that my mum has not fallen prey to a killer, one such that has delighted my senses but now sends terror into my being.

How would he have killed her? Please don't let me see the technicolour scenes that live in my memory. My wee mum, I often dreamed of finding her body in some wooded area where I would bury her properly and lovingly lay her to rest and erect a cross with her name carved on it. I had nightmares, picturing animals chewing at her flesh, and once more I asked God to help us find her.

One day, in a fit of rage at myself, I gathered up all my DVDs of horrors, and I threw them in a skip outside someone's house. This was my entire fault. I had brought a curse on my home with all the trash I had watched. I had brought this horror into our lives; my DVDs brought the movies to reality. Reality was my mum still missing and I had to go back to it and live in it even though it was slowly drowning my mind in its filth.

CHAPTER 5

I went back to school, and it was worse than I thought it would be. I was prepared for my friends' concern and my enemies' scorn, but I wasn't ready for the silence that my presence generated when I approached people. I discovered the headmaster had instructed that no one was to mention my mum to me. I could have dealt with the curiosity, but this silence unnerved me. My teachers treated me with kid gloves, but the pity in their eyes never let me forget that I was different.

Break and lunch times were an ordeal that I had to live through. Gone were the happy breaks that made school bearable, and how I missed my friends who tried so hard to be friends, but friendship had gone to be replaced with uncomfortable silences or dialogues filled with mindless trash when all my buddies watched every word that they uttered, just in case they mentioned the dreaded words—gone, missing, murdered, adultery, mum, or even family—that set us apart. I was the boy whose mum was missing, presumed murdered by his dad. They meant well, but it was finished, over. I would have preferred to be left alone to nurse my hurt and bewilderment.

I could practically see the burden of me lift off their shoulders when we parted. I know they met up without telling me, but you know what, I did not blame them; I would be the same in their shoes. I assumed that most people had written my mum off; they thought she was dead. I always thought we were an ordinary family, an ordinary boring family that nothing much happened to. Now we are the talk of the town, and people speculate about what happened to our mum.

Most people avoid us, especially our friends, who have mysteriously disappeared. How many times had I wanted to be famous? Now, I would gladly welcome anonymity. All I want is to be Tom, son of Rina, who is at home waiting for Tom, waiting like she always was, with a cup of hot chocolate and numerous chocolate biscuits. I close my eyes, and I can picture the scene, and I remember how my mum would ask me questions that bored me to tears. I used to answer in a dismissive way and run up the stairs as she followed me, trying to show that she was interested in her son's life. I was only interested in getting upstairs to view my precious DVDs.

Mum, I would stay at the table, and I would talk to you, really talk to you, and I would ask about your day and we would laugh about silly things, just like we did when I was little before I became the son who brushed you off preferring a trashy movie. Mum, I love you. Please come home. I will change, I love you.

I think about random things like being grateful that my mum's mum and dad are dead and that she was an only child, so her family are spared the heartache that we have. My dad's mum lives too far away and has escaped the news about Mum. Dad has told her some concocted story about them separating, but she is so far gone in her mind that she has accepted this tale, another person who can easily forget my mum, sometimes it is as if Mum has never lived or breathed. Is it only me who misses her?

CHAPTER 6

I go into her bedroom when Dad is not about. I touch her belongings, I gather her clothes about me, and I smell them; and soon I am bawling my eyes out with an anguish I did not believe I was capable of feeling. I carry a pain about in my chest that makes it hard for me to breathe.

Today, when Ricky called, I showed him our family photo albums, and he told me he felt like he already knew my mum personally because I had talked about her so much. He thought she looked beautiful in her photos, and he made me see my mum as a person in her own right as well as my mum. Ricky encouraged me, and he helped me to stick my mum's photos, especially the photos of me with Mum up on my bedroom wall. I like that Mum's face is the last thing I see before I go to sleep at night. Why is it that I can talk to Ricky about Mum and yet I can't talk to my dad or sister? They rarely mention Mum, but Ricky talks about her all the time. Life is so strange, no one is the same.

I dread going to bed at night. I have nightmares now. They start as lovely, soothing dreams. I am in Mum's arms, and I see her smiling face as she gazes down at me. She is swinging me round and round by the hands. I am holding her hands for dear life, and I am squealing with delight mixed with fear. I remember her playing with me like this, and I recall the fear, but I also remember how I would gaze into her soft grey eyes and the love I saw reflected there reassured me that I was perfectly safe in my mum's arms, so I would demand more and more until Mum and I, giggling uncontrollably, would fall exhausted together unto the sofa.

In my dream, I actually feel her arms about me, and I smell her perfume as she swings me round and round. But suddenly, she disappears, and I reach for her hands, screaming 'Mum', but she is gone, so I fall to the floor, and I wake up sobbing and drenched in sweat.

Most of my nights are like this, and I yearn and dread them in equal measure. I close my eyes, and I pray for the feel of her arms about me. A feeling of peace engulfs me when a beautiful memory plays its poignant tune across my heart, but it always ends far too soon, and the feeling of desolation I experience breaks me. Most days, I waken in a bed soaked in tears.

CHAPTER 7

Our first Christmas without our lovely mum, and I spent it in tears of self-pity and unbearable remorse. I fought with Dad over everything: Should we have a tree? Should we have presents? Should we be even a bit happy?

How could I know what to be or do? I even shouted at Ricky because he had a strange-looking Christmas tree up in the window of his bedroom and the twinkling lights nearly drove me to run up his stairs and destroy the tree, but he talked me into putting lights on the tree in our side garden next to his house. 'Lights', he said, 'would welcome Mum if she came home.'

I hated those lights, and on Christmas day, in a fit of impotent fury, I tore them down and ripped them to shreds, shredding my hands on the bulbs in the process. Ricky bathed my bloody fingers and listened as I rambled on about our Christmases in the past. I probably made them out to be the best Christmases any family ever had, but to me, that's how I remember them.

Oh, my mum, where are you? You must be dead because you would never stay away at Christmas. You loved it. Memories torture me, and a kaleidoscope of pictures flows through my mind, and I am desolate. I remember every Christmas, and I can conjure them up to inflict more pain on my heart. The Christmas I got my first bike and how Mum held the back as I struggled to learn to ride it myself. Dad soon gave up, but Mum held that bike until she knew I was safe. I knew she had hurt her back, but I didn't even thank her. Oh, Mum! The pride and concern on her face when I got a 'big bike' and raced off down the road.

I took it for granted that my mum was happy, but was she? Is it too late to tell her how thankful I am, thankful for the everyday things, the Christmas things, even stirring the fruit pudding, and then I remember how I refused to join in. Memories of not too pleasant things, shame, at the times when I said, 'Mum, grow up, I have,' when she wanted to read *The Night before Christmas* and *The First Christmas*, and I refused to stir the pudding, I refused to help clean the car, and oh the shame of how I showed my impatience when she tried to tell me about the centre — her centre. I wasn't interested. I did not find her interesting. Is that why she went to the centre, and did she think we did not love her? How I tortured myself with this line of thinking, but I knew if my mum came home, I would gladly stand in her kitchen and listen to her talking forever while I gladly stirred any pudding she wanted to make, and the wishes we made together would all come true.

CHAPTER 8

My birthday. Now, I know my mum is dead. A pit is slowly opening before me, a dark deep pit, which I know I am tipping into. It is only a matter of when I will fall in and disappear, just like Mum.

Ricky lets me talk about Mum all the time, which I find hard to do with Dad, because I know Dad feels guilty about cheating on her. He never mentions her, and now that a year has gone past, neither does Lucy; she is infatuated with this new boyfriend and stays at his house most of the time now. Dad allows it because it suits him. He can go see Susan whenever he likes. Dad can't or won't deal with me, so he encourages Ricky to call as often as he likes. I am not sorry. I can relate to Ricky. There are far too many raw emotions simmering beneath my relationship with my dad. He is wrapped up in his new life with Susan. How I hate that woman! I am starting to hate Dad too. I heard him whistling as he splashed aftershave on his ugly, cheating face. I hoped he would cut his own throat.

Dad, Lucy, and I had a blazing row today, and I could not find Ricky to help me. Dad decided to put all of Mum's clothes and belongings into the garage. He thought it time we laid Mum and her belongings to rest. He is a bastard. How can he even think of doing this? He was even talking about having a memorial for Mum with just the family to say a farewell to her. Farewell to her? I wanted to say hello to her. He said we needed closure, and he nearly got closure of a different kind when I went for him, and I would have choked him had Lucy not hit me on the arm with the poker. I was incensed and thankfully to her credit, so was Lucy. What would Mum do if she came home and found her things gone? She would think we did not love her. Thankfully, Dad realised how strong our feelings about this were, so he backed down and agreed to swap rooms with me as long as I removed all the photos of Mum from my walls.

How could he forget Mum so easily and try to eradicate all traces of her from our home? I could not believe how heartless my dad was being, and I wondered if my dad had always been this cold? He definitely was not the man I had thought he was, and I could not help wondering if this is how he would be if I had gone missing instead of Mum. I know my mum would search for me all the rest of her life. I knew how much she loved me. She would not give up, and she would keep my bedroom just the way it was when I went missing. Guiltily, I wished it were Dad who was missing.

Thankfully, I had Ricky to talk to, and he gave me the affection that I craved but did not get from my dad. He helped me move rooms. Nothing was too much trouble for him, and I was amazed by the way he gently handled Mum's clothing and seemed to caress them. He really was a comforting and true, understanding friend; I imagined how my old friends would have reacted in the same circumstances. They would have run a mile and dropped me like a hot potato.

Surrounded by my mum's belongings and her face smiling down on me from the pictures I, with Ricky's help, had stuck up on the walls, I felt close to her, and her perfume comforted me as I lay with my face on her nightie, and it acted like a drug to my senses and sent me to sleep. Gradually, the perfume started to fade, and I sprayed more and more on my bed until my friends in school joked that I was turning into a fairy because they could smell Mum's perfume off my clothes.

One night when I struggled to sleep, I searched for Mum's perfume, but I could not find it. I ended up in a frenzy, and I was taking the room apart when Dad appeared and demanded to know what all the noise was about. I told him I could not find Mum's perfume, and when Dad told me he had got so sick of the smell that he threw the perfume out. I vaguely remember grabbing him, pushing him out of my bedroom, and slamming the door in his face, and no matter how many times he said he was sorry, I knew I would never forgive him. I screamed that it was Ricky's aftershave that he could smell, lavender. I hated it myself, but Ricky seemed to love it, and soon our house seemed to smell just like him. I emptied the bin all over the garden the next morning, but Mum's perfume was gone, just like her.

Lucy kept washing my sheets, and soon, Mum's soothing perfume was gone forever. I found that I couldn't get to sleep until I was totally exhausted, and I lived in a fog of tiredness. I rarely spoke to my dad, but I had to know the name of Mum's perfume. I planned to buy it, and in doing so, I thought it would be the answer to my insomnia. I thought Dad was lying when he told me he could not remember the name of Mum's perfume. Lucy did not know it either, and I thought this spoke volumes about the interest we had had in our mum. How could they not know what perfume she liked? But I was as guilty as the other two.

I nearly got thrown out of the department store for opening all the bottles of perfume to smell them. It took me weeks and cost me, or rather Dad, a fortune, but he did not complain. I think he was frightened of my manic behaviour and frightened of my strength because I had grown a lot in the past year and I could not wait to see the pride on Mum's face when she saw me.

With the heady smell of Mum's perfume once again permeating everything I owned, I at first felt better in myself, but soon, I found it hard to get to sleep at night again because I dreaded the nightmares, which were getting steadily worse. The perfume was losing its magic, and I tried and tried, but I could not feel my mum's presence around me anymore and the feeling of desolation was unbearable. I walked the floor every night until the small hours feeling abandoned and horribly alone.

CHAPTER 9

Most nights, I would see a light on in Ricky's house, so I guessed he did not sleep well either. I could not believe that Mum had been gone a full year. The police informed us that sometimes this yearly anniversary triggers something in the missing person. They feel the need to contact home and say they are well. If they are still alive, they might get in touch with their family.

I waited patiently by the phone for a full week, but nothing happened and finally my heart broke, broke into a million tiny pieces and each piece seemed to show a picture of Mum and I, pictures that swam before my eyes but stayed completely out of my grasp. She was gone, and I had to start to try and live without her, but I couldn't.

I found I could not sleep for more than a few hours every night and I could not eat much before I was sick. I rarely washed or changed my clothes; another bone of contention, I did not care. Why should I? The house was in as bad a state as I was. Who cared? Dad certainly didn't; Lucy tried, but she had been brought up thinking she was above dirt and she didn't 'do' cleaning. Dad, I realised was a lazy git. Mum had done everything, so why should he change? He was waiting until he could move Susan in; she was to be his 'help'. I did not feel sorry for her. She had made her own bed.

I rowed every time Dad left to visit Susan, thinking that this time he would bring her back with him. I screamed that he had killed our mum so many times that Lucy fell apart. She could take no more and left home. At least, we knew where she was, living in her boyfriend's home with his rich parents. Lucy was another one lost to me. I am alone, desperately alone, in a house with no foundation, no walls, no nothing.

CHAPTER 10

I woke up in the hospital. In a mental hospital, believe it or not. I find it hard to believe. Dad had found me unconscious; he thought I had taken an overdose or something, but I had just collapsed with lack of food and sleep. I was glad to be out of the house, but I was terrified that I would miss Mum if she somehow came home. What if I missed her and she disappeared again. I became frantic until Dad promised that he would stay in the house until I was well enough to go home. I panicked that she might return when Dad was at work so, treacherous pig, he moved Susan in, just what he wanted, but someone had to watch for Mum.

I gradually calmed down; the hospital was quiet, and the staff were really great. The doctors told me I had suffered a mental breakdown. A psychiatrist talked to me for hours and let me ramble on and on about my wonderful mum. This helped me enormously. He told me I was not to blame myself for Mum's disappearance. I listened intently to him, this good kind man, but he didn't know my mum. He didn't know the damage done to my heart. I smiled, I listened, but my heart was broken into a million pieces, fragments that reflected years, weeks, and days of my life, my life with my mum. He helped me piece the fragments together, but a broken vessel is still broken. The cracks are always there, waiting to fall apart at the next trauma.

Ricky visited me. He was the one to help me see that I had to move on. He told me to hold my mum in my heart but to live the way she would like me to and be happy. He reached me when no one else did; he knew me so well. I started to eat properly, and I soon got well again, well on the outside, but on the inside, I was just burying my thoughts. On the surface, I seemed calm, I was calm enough to go home, I was cured, but they were very wrong. They should have looked more carefully into my eyes. The dark desolation that dwelt therein would have told them how sick I was. I would never be well again.

When I eventually went home, Ricky was the one to pull the whole family together and insisted we speak to each other. Ricky made me realise that Dad and Lucy had moved on with their lives and I had to as well. I did not like it, but as there was nothing I could do about it, I agreed.

I rebelled at Susan moving into our home. I ranted, I raved, but I was overruled. I know Susan tried everything that she could to get me to like her, but I just could not forgive her for loving my dad and taking his affection away from my mum. I still blamed her for whatever had happened to Mum, but an uneasy truce had fallen on our home.

We lived together as strangers, and I plotted how I would get rid of Dad and Susan when I was older and then I would wait for Mum to come home. I would remove all traces of Susan from this house, and I would return it to the way it was when mum disappeared. So I studied every room, and when Susan replaced anything, I knew right away. I refused to allow them to throw anything away. Rows upon rows followed until they agreed to store everything in the garage. Soon, the garage looked like my home, and my home became Susan's. My mum will go mad when she sees all her things stuck in the garage. Mum's things are lovely, comfortingly familiar and dear to my heart. Susan's are modern and shiny, but they are not familiar and comforting, and Susan thinks I do not know what she is up to. You, Susan, are thick. I know you are trying to eradicate Mum from the house, but it can all be put back in an instant, when mum returns. Now, I have another shrine to Mum, and I sit here most nights, dreaming that I am sitting watching TV with my mum.

CHAPTER 11

Lucy was to be married, and Dad wanted her married from her own home. By this time, it did not even remotely look like her old home. Susan had wrought miracles; the messy dirty home we, Dad, Lucy, and myself had created in the wake of Mum's disappearance had been transformed into a show house. I was past caring; I had my old home safely wrapped up in love in our garage, clean and tidy, just waiting for my mum.

I could not get caught up in the wedding preparations, but Ricky amazed me by being in the middle of it all. He asked umpteen questions about Mum that Susan went off in a huff, which pleased me no end. It was Ricky who suggested Lucy should wear Mum's own wedding dress, and it was a good choice because she looked beautiful in it. I was pleased to see a tear in Dad's eye, and I liked to imagine that he remembered his and Mum's own wedding day. I was annoyed to see the look Ricky bestowed on my sister, and I rowed with him over it, but he roared with laughter and soon we were friends again.

On Lucy's wedding day, she stood in the living room, Susan's living room, resplendent in her finery, and I tried to summon up some affection for my sister, but when I noticed the soft white roses of her bouquet, I closed my eyes, for the sight was so painful I nearly fell to my knees. But I could still see them emblazoned on my eyelids. White roses, Mum's favourite flowers! I had forgotten just how much she loved them. I saw myself as a tiny boy carrying a huge bunch of these up the stairs, and the memory was so sharp I smelt their perfume as the petals tickled my nose — my mum's face, youthful and full of love and her strong hands as she lifted me up on to the bed and into her arms and the petals of the roses all around us.

I struggled to breathe, I wanted to run and run, and I wanted to take the roses out of my sister's hands and beat my dad and sister to death with them. I opened my eyes, and I looked at the roses prayed my sister would prick her finger on a thorn and bleed all over her white dress, Mum's dress, and the blood would be our tears for Mum. I did not remember walking to the car and getting in to it. My mind was swirling in a sea of betrayal and anger. Stop this pretence at a normal family, stop the farce, stop this acting, we are not normal. Why are we doing normal things, like a wedding? Our mother is missing. We should be waiting for her to return before we do family things. The whole world should stop until Mum comes home. How can it go on as normal?

They pretended everything was normal, but they did not know of the unbearable grief I felt and the terrible anger I harboured at the betrayal of my mother. How could Lucy look so beautiful and happy? How could Dad gaze into the eyes of Susan and smile? How could Susan take the place of my poor mum? I could not, for the life of me, comprehend how they could do this. My heart felt bruised, and I clenched my hands at my sides and I dug my nails into my hands until I drew blood, just to stop me from shouting out loudly in the church, 'Stop. We need to wait until Mum is here. We can't do this without Mum.'

I felt my tie, this stupid gold cravat, begin to choke me, and I pulled at it as the sweat trickled down my back. I knew I was hyperventilating, but I was powerless to stop it, and as I heard my heart pounding and my mind go spinning out of control in a vortex of pulsating red blood, I heard the minister ask if anyone knew of anything to prevent this union. I opened my mouth to scream 'yes, I do', but nothing came out. My mouth was dry, and all accusations were banging about in my head.

I started to shake and tremor; I was hot then suddenly cold. Why can I not speak? I tried to stand, but my legs had lost their power. My head fell forward as a huge sob rose in my throat. I knew I was going to do something outrageous, then I felt a hand cover my hand. I looked down at the hand covering mine, and it became more than a hand. It became my salvation; all the panic, hatred, and sickness I was feeling flooded into that hand, and I knew when I looked up into the eyes of the person whose hand covered mine I would find understanding and love. There he stood — Ricky. I knew he cared for me. I had him to love; I needed no one else, and I wanted no one else. I had been left, abandoned, betrayed, and abused by my family. No more will I flounder and be lonely. I was lost, but now, I have been found. Oh, Ricky, I love you. Thank you for always being there. I felt a rush of love course through me, and I instantly calmed down. I had Ricky. The rest of my family could go to hell; I did not need them. Ricky would be here for me just like he was here for me when Mum disappeared. I would let my sister and my dad go, I would easily forget them, I had Ricky, and he had me.

Ricky

'Happy Christmas, lavender girl. What would you like me to buy you? Now, you know I hate to see that look in your eyes. "You better watch out you better not cry, you better watch out I'm telling you why Santa Claus is coming tonight, he knows just when you're happy, he knows just when you're sad, he knows when you're good, and he knows just when you're bad." I know what we need in here. Be back in a minute.'

RINA

CHAPTER 1

Tears slowly fall as I poignantly recall singing that song to my children, and I prayed that my family would have a happy Christmas. My thoughts and prayers would be of them, and even though I could not be with them, I had years of memories that I would bring out and savour. I would start with our very first Christmas before we had the children right up to last year, and I felt blessed with the mountainous, beautiful memories I had to enjoy.

As I recalled the memories I had stored, I could almost feel my family with me. Steve dressed as Santa. I giggled as I pictured the makeshift Santa suit and how we got tipsy and tripped up the stairs, shushing each other in loud whispers as we tried not to waken the children. Tom as a baby, his first bike, and Steve trying to ride it down the street after he had blown up the tyres at the garage. He was still slightly drunk after his work Christmas party, and the sight of him with his legs sticking out made me laugh. The terror still fills my heart when I remember Tom's first big bike and how I worried. Lucy and her dolls—I am amazed that I can remember each one. I even remember the dresses I made for them, and I think of the Christmas Eve nights when I gladly sat up until the wee hours finishing off my gifts to my beloved children. Happy, happy days, the memories that this monster cannot rob me of.

My children's legs, their chubby little legs that I loved to kiss, both children tucked up in bed, angelic faces calm and dreamy. How I used to long for bedtime when they were small, and I was constantly tired. Now, I would treasure each moment of every day: their first day at school and how it was me who cried, me who was lonely, me who felt that the days were too long. We do not know what a day brings.

All my 'mother's days' come rushing by: chocolates, flowers, white roses clutched in chubby little arms, cards made with dirty little hands, dirty little hands that made me mad when they left dirty little handprints on my clean windows and mirrors. I would never clean my windows if I could go back and have those dirty little hands once more. Hold those dirty little precious hands; feel them clutch my hands as we crossed the roads. Who will hold their hands now? If they are frightened or sad, who will hold their hands? Steve, you had better love them, love them until I can come home. Dirty little hands that became young adult hands that could do things for themselves. They did not need me, but I was so happy to see them grow. I want them back. I want those happy years back so that I can wallow in their happiness, wallow and swallow them up greedily and stuff my heart full to the brim.

CHAPTER 2

Soft fur . . . soft fur brushes against my leg, and a memory arises in my mind—cat. Oh, cat, you have found me, you have not forgotten me. My cat has come to bring me comfort; her soft fur is so soothing as she rubs herself against my legs. What are you thinking, cat, as you see me here? Can you sense my fear and heartache? Can you go and fetch my family and lead them to me? I know you could do this. If you come here all the time, Tom will follow you, and he will find me. Please, cat, go before he sees you. Go fetch Tom. Oh no, here he comes with a bulging stocking in his arms.

'What have we here? A visitor? My, my, here, pussy, pussy, we can't have visitors here now, can we? Here, pussy, pussy, my love, what a beautiful pussy you are.'

No, no, he is going to harm my cat. Not my poor cat. She has come for me. Run, cat, run, and unbelievably, she does, as fast as lightening. So fast, he falls flat on his face as he lunges for her. My eyes light up in anticipation. Cat will show my family where I am held.

'You stupid woman, do you think cats are like dogs? No one is going to follow a cat, especially when I close the window, she climbed in through. She will never get back inside again, so get that hopeful look off your face. You are mine now, and you will always be mine.'

He hangs the stocking on my contraption, and he wraps a set of Christmas lights all around me, artistically arranging them, then switching them on, and I sparkle and twinkle, and he places me directly in front of the window. Can't you see me? Can no one see me? I'm all lit up.

'That's better. A bit of Christmas cheer. You look well dressed as a Christmas tree. Saved me some money. Do you like your stocking? You will later, or I will. I'm afraid I spent more money than I should have, but the toys were hard for me to resist. Now, don't look at me like that again. I'm promising you we will have some fun with these. Did I tell you Tom is coming for Christmas dinner? Ha, not pleased? His acceptance brought a smile to my face.'

My tormentor teases me with more torture. Can't you see me? You will if you just look up. One Christmas full of goodwill and cheer, but my Christmas full of heartache and fear.

CHAPTER 3

I look in the mirror, and I wonder who this old lady is who is always looking back at me. She never speaks; she can't speak because she always wears a piece of duct tape across her mouth. I would like to have a conversation with her. I would tell her that I am doing as well as can be expected considering the circumstances I find myself in. I want to tell her that she has lost far too much weight and that she had better try to eat more or she will get sick and die. I would tell her that she does not look well, so thin, and that she looked much younger the first time I saw her.

I remember the first time I saw her. It seems like yesterday, and yet, it also seems as long as death. She was pretty with shiny dark hair cut fashionably short. Her teeth were good and white, and her skin glowed with a healthy tan. Her eyes, well, her eyes, were full of terror, but now, now, they are full of nothing. I guessed she liked to keep fit, but what has happened to her? The woman before me is as pale as death with skin covered in unhealthy marks. She has hardly any teeth, and her hair hangs limply down over her skinny shoulders. I wish she would dye it. The grey does nothing for her. It just makes her look old and haggard, and I know she is not old. In fact, she is not yet fifty. I wish she would look after herself better. I hate it when women let themselves go. If they have no respect for themselves, then no one else will either.

What did he just say? Lucy is getting married today. Lucy? My Lucy? No, she is too young; she is a little girl. What age is she now? I look out the window, this window that I both hate and treasure. This window, that has kept me from dying. This window, that I have looked through each day and watched as my family live their lives without me. I have watched the seasons come and go with intensity that I never had before. I have absorbed with great satisfaction everything I have witnessed. I am greedy, very greedy for more, much more. I am never full, never satisfied. I want and need more of everything I see.

How much they have changed! Will they forgive how much I am changed? A little voice questions how I can ask this unanswerable question. I thirst for sight of any one of them and then I cry huge buckets of tears when I do see them. Can't you see me? Can't you see me? Why?

I see my beautiful daughter walk down our path holding on to her dad's arm. Lucy is wearing my wedding dress, the dress I wore on one of the happiest days of my life, and I think of my parents. My heart is heavy with remembered faces that swim in and out of my vision, faces that wished me happiness on my wedding day, and I was happy and I will be happy again one day. One day, when all this ugliness is safely behind me, I will be happy. Who am I trying to kid?

Lucy is carrying a bunch of white roses, my favourites. Tears, I thought I had no tears left, but I have hot scalding tears that burn my face and sear my heart. My daughter is getting married today, and I can't be there. How many times had I dreamed of this day, and how many plans had I made over the years when Lucy was growing up? I remember the game we used to play on rainy days. I would draw your bridesmaids with their pretty dresses but make sure that your picture of yourself as a bride would be far prettier than mine. How many dresses did we draw, and as I close my eyes, pictures of you in lots of white dresses float before me and soon my eyes are wet with tears once more. Lucy in her Christening robe, your first white dress, all the other pretty white dresses you wore float by my face, but you have disappeared. I shake my head, but the dresses are still there, dresses, lots of pretty white dresses, and suddenly, you are there and you are smiling.

My little girl and the hopes and dreams I wished for you. I know you are happy today, my Lucy. Please don't let me be a spectre at your wedding feast. Think of me and remember the love I have for you and smile at my memory. I wish the world for you, and I pray God keeps you safe and that you find love and contentment in your husband. This man whom you have chosen, may he bring you happiness, may he be kind and honourable, may he never treat you like this man treats me.

I look at this woman who has taken my place. She is dressed as the mother of the bride, and I hate her. Susan, I would not have chosen blue. It makes you look washed out and bland. I know I am being unreasonable, but my soul cries out at the injustice of my life. I should be there. I am the mother of the bride. You, Susan, you will never take my place. When I am back with my family, I will get rid of you. You will go quicker than you came. I will erase every trace of you out of my family, and you will be no more. Steve, you are taking photos. How could you, when I am not there? Never worry, we can take new ones with the real mother of the bride in centre stage.

Pain, as I realise, my Lucy, that I missed your last night at home as our little girl. How I would have loved to have spent hours with you, my little girl all grown up! I would have washed your long blond hair until it squeaked and brushed it not one hundred times but thousands, until it shone like gold. I would have talked to you of wisdom in marriage and held you in my arms as you slept the last sleep of a young girl, and I would have cried rivers of tears when you walked down the aisle as a woman. Most of all, I missed telling you how proud I am of you and how much I love you. Now, two are gone from our home, but a cuckoo has moved in. Build your own nest, Susan. You shan't have mine!

He laughs so hard it pierces my head. Then he tells me that he is going to the wedding. He has been invited to keep Tom company, and he explains in graphic detail just how he would really like to keep Tom company. I look at this small nondescript man, and for the first time since I have been a prisoner, I let him see the total contempt I have for him in my eyes. He sees the change in me, and he is excited. I have ignited his interest in me again.

'Such a pity I can't stay and enjoy your mood, but Tom awaits me and you are not going anywhere, are you? I will take lots of photos and we can look at them together later and I might just bring you some wedding cake back. I'm sure wedding cake tastes just as good liquidised.'

I am left alone to think and cry, cry for the woman who was Rina.

RICKY

Chapter 1

A typical wedding. Well, almost, it is my first special wedding, in fact my first wedding at all. Weddings, they are to legalise sex. I don't need a wedding to have sex, especially with my Rina, but what a thought, and I fantasise about dressing Rina up in her own wedding dress. A wedding has to have witnesses and guests. I have my bride, and I nearly have my witness. Could I, could I really pull it off? Could I have my two? Or let's not leave Susan out of the equation. She has shown herself quite up to erotic behaviour, three guests. My mind fills with this tantalising tableau. Could I do it? Of course, I could. I can do anything with this disgusting family. What a journey I am about to travel! What experiences I have yet to devour! I can hardly contain myself as I plan and scheme for their downfall.

I know I have the bold Tom eating out of my hand. Whom will I pick next? Lucy, she will be the easiest. Her husband, I will leave alone. I feel nothing for him; he is colourless. Lucy is bright red and just waiting; she will be easy. Susan? Well, what can I say about Susan? She will get special treatment because she hurt my Rina. Steve, he is weak, but he is a man. Ah, am I afraid of Steve? I have to think a bit about Steve, but I will have him in the end. This is great. I will have them all, and who will ever know, who will even care? I will be so thorough. I will be so careful. What a delightful time Rina and I are going to have planning this reception. I need to order more contraptions, but I won't need more beds. People will puzzle, but in the end, they will be glad to be shot of this family that embarrasses their community. I will make sure that people will think the family has done a moonlit flit; people do it all the time. Then the gossip will really begin. The thoughts they had kept to themselves will be brought to the surface and voiced. The family went because something really fishy did go on in that house. People will start to remember things that never happened in the first place, but now, they remember, oh, so clearly.

I shiver with delight and I look at all the guests gathered in this church and I know exactly what they are thinking. First of all, I know they are thinking how this family can have an ordinary wedding in the circumstances. Then they think of Rina, and I also think of the lovely Rina, the Rina I have just left in her dark hole. I hope she is hungry, I hope she is dirty, and I hope and pray she is tortured by her memories of this awful family. Ah, you are aghast that I pray. Well, I do but what God answers my prayers.

I know I am a monster, but I am happy being a monster. How boring to live a 'normal' life! I wake each day not knowing what surprises life has in store for me. I am never bored. Well, I was once when I was about six, I think. They put me in a mental hospital, the cheek of them, a mental hospital. I am not mental. I am evil, bad, and manipulative, a monster definitely, but I am certainly not mad.

I think of my parents sometimes, but they are like strangers to me now and I can't remember any tenderness they might have bestowed on me. I found them weak and unremarkable. My dad was a very tall, well-built man who carried about with him an aura of gentleness, which infuriated me. I wish I had had his height and strength. I would have used them well. *My* dad stared at me with his soft brown eyes all the time as if he could not quite believe what he saw. My dad saw me do it, and he tried to understand the enormity of my actions.

It was my dad who had me put away, but on the day they came for me, he held me close and he cried and he cried 'My son, my son, why did you do it?' How I cried and cried and acted so distraught that I soon had the doctors eating out of my hand. The fools, they are beyond my contempt. I very soon had them believing my dad was the one who might need help and that I could not be capable of this horrendous crime. Whoever paid for their university degrees was robbed and cheated, doctors of the mind. They should have been in jail for their thievery. I was so well behaved that they let me out in a few weeks, and I know they thought my dad had imagined that I had pushed my twin sister out of the bedroom window. How I would love to be a fly on the wall when these educated doctors next discuss me, if only they knew the real me!

Chapter 2

I have always hated my sister. Let me tell you why, although I have no need to explain myself. But you might want to put your own slant on it, not that I am interested. I gave up wondering what people thought of me years ago. My mum wheeled us about in a twin pram, a navy blue Silver Cross pram, which brought tears to my eyes the first time I saw its beautiful lines, but my mother put my sister at the top end, facing her, and I was at the bottom end, looking at my sister.

I know they smiled at each other over my head, and I know they laughed at their secret jokes. They laughed at me and made fun of my clothes. My sister was dressed in such beautiful soft and silky clothes and the hats, oh how I ached to wear those hats, but no, I was dressed in hard brown itchy clothes. I was ashamed to be seen in my clothes, and my mum and sister were ashamed of me. That is the reason why I was placed in the bottom of the pram, practically hidden by the hood and handle. It was all I could do to stop myself from biting the lilywhite treacherous hands that pushed us.

People would stop and admire my sister, and I have to admit she was lovely with her pretty pink clothes and the soft white ribbon in her blond curls. They would coo and say, 'Isn't she gorgeous?' And then I would wait for it with my heart in my mouth, for their startled looks and their, 'Oh, he's a serious little one, isn't he?' I suppose the frown on my face did not help, but I had heard the disparaging remarks too often to try to smile because what had I to smile about? My mum loved my sister more than she did me. Why else would she dress her so that people would stop and admire her and then dress me so badly that people pitied me my plainness? I knew I was prettier than my sister, but I was at a disadvantage because of the way my mum dressed me.

I stiffened with anger when complete strangers suggested my sister looked like my mother. How dare they? Were they blind? I wanted to look like my mother. I desired the blond curly hair and the dark blue eyes. If looks could kill, these strangers would have dropped dead at the side of our pram. Instead, they ignored my dark-filled face and smiled benignly at my sister's sunny countenance. I vowed they would pay for my hurt, every one of them. I wriggled and thrashed about in the pram so much trying to dislodge my fat sister on to the ground that I ended up looking worse than ever, hair everywhere and clothes resembling a jumble sale. I could kill them all. I managed to kick my sister a few times, but Mum put a pillow between our feet, thus hampering my actions.

I got my revenge even at such a young age. I bit my mum's nipple so hard that I drew blood. How good that made me feel! But Mum did worse. She stopped breastfeeding me and gave me a bottle. A bottle? Woman, what were you about? Breast milk is best, but I was in for a bigger shock. I was heartbroken when I saw my mum feed my sister, and I refused to take the horrible bottle of cow's milk offered to me.

I refused to eat for nearly a week, and I enjoyed seeing the distress my mum was in. She deserved it, refusing me her breasts. Nurses and then doctors came and prodded me, and I quite enjoyed the attention I was receiving until they stuck me in the hospital, and I knew the time had not arrived, for I was too young to achieve all that I desired. I knew I had to play smart until I could look after myself, so I sucked so hard and earnestly at my bottles that I was soon at home and in the loving embrace of my family once again.

My victory was tarnished; my mum only bottle-fed me when my dad was not around to do it, but she lovingly cuddled my sister to her voluptuous breasts, and to my fury, she hummed as she breastfed her. How my blood boiled to see my fat sister with my mother's white frothy milk running down her chin and to witness my sister knead my mother's breast with her chubby hand just as if it belonged to her. I tried to cuddle into my mum, but I always felt her stiffen when I nuzzled her breast to seek out her milk. I could not help it. The smell of her milk nearly drove me insane, and to be denied, it was slow torture for me. I threw tantrum after tantrum, and I screamed and screamed until I threw up.

'Colic,' the doctor said. I had colic, and wasn't it fortunate that mum had only one boy because boys were prone to colic? If I had a pound for every time mum was told she was lucky to have her precious little angel of a daughter, I would be rich. I did not have colic. Could my mum not see I was just feeling unloved? I wanted to be dressed in the pretty pastel clothes with the fluffy white hat and to sit at the top of the pram. I wanted to be admired by the people, but most of all, I wanted to be the one looking at my mum's face and to see her smile at me, not my sister. If we had been given turns in the top of the pram, I might have turned out different, but then again, I don't want to be different. I like the way I am.

CHAPTER 3

My sister hated me. She hated me since we were born. Did she hate me in the womb? Did we war and fight for supremacy even inside our mother? I can't remember, but from the first moment I set eyes on my fat sister, I knew I hated her with a vengeance. She should not have been. I should have been one. My mother had only enough love for one, and that should have been me. I know why I hated her. Why did she hate me? Was it because I nipped and pinched her any chance I got. I knew where her soft places were, and I nipped so hard that she screamed, which made me giggle. She was a telltale, and I received numerous punishments for my treatment of her.

My dad worked in an accountant's; he was not a fully qualified accountant, typical of him, I thought, always runner-up, never a leader. In my mind, Dad should have owned the office, not just worked there. It offended my sense of worth. When my sister was a toddler, she would wait at our gate for Dad coming home, and all my misdemeanours would be catalogued for him. Dinnertime became a war zone as I fought for supremacy in gaining my parents attention over and above my sister. I failed miserably, so I took my revenge by beating my sister up. Mother grew so distracted with us that she became ill, and I was elated because I had overheard Dad say that he was going to get Mother some help with the children, and I thought I would at last get my mother to myself. Halleluiah, I had won. Help would look after Sister.

My lovely, Mother gave me over to the helper while she—I can hardly even say it now all these years later—took my sister to the park, leaving me behind. I could hardly believe it as I watched her set off holding tightly to my sister's fat hand. My eyes blazed with fury at the injustice of it. I stewed for hours, waiting for them to return, and then it would be my turn. I would be so good and pleasant that my mother would have a better time at the park with me than she had had with my sister! I even washed my face and hands, and I stole chocolate out of the kitchen to present to my mother. We would share it while we walked in the park. We would stay for hours and hours, and we would be so late home that sister would be in bed, put there by the help.

Can you imagine the anger I felt when my mother and sister returned, my mother carrying my sleeping sister and informing the help to take me to the park because my mother was too tired after carrying my lazy fat sister? I refused to go, and I threw such a tantrum, kicking and screaming, but the helper dragged me up of the floor and bodily carried me to the park, where I behaved so badly, throwing stones at the ducks and kicking any child that unwittingly strayed near me, that my minder grabbed my hand and trailed me home.

At home, I was so incensed to find my sister asleep in my mum's arms that I flew at her and I bit her on her leg so hard that she woke up, screamed and then lost her breath, and turned blue. She deserved it, the traitorous wee liar. She had planned it and planned it well. I knew my mother had cuddled my sister in her lap, and I guessed she had sung a sweet lullaby to her before she had kissed her head a thousand times as my sister had fallen asleep. If I closed my eyes, I could picture it, but I pictured it with me on my mother's knee instead of my sister.

It was the first time my dad had ever struck me, and it hurt. He was furious, but I was so enraged that I bit my sister again, so my dad hit me on the legs once more, and as I went for my sister again, my dad lifted me bodily of the floor and forced my hands behind my back. He tied them together with his belt, but I was so far gone that this did not stop me. I ran for my sister and bit her again, so my dad grabbed me and wrestled me to the floor, and he tied my legs together with another belt. I tried to roll across the floor, but it was too hard, so I lay there screaming and kicking and threatening all sorts of vengeance on my tormenters. The faces that stared back at me were full of horror and shock, which only made me worse, especially my stupid sister's face. She had her thumb stuck in her mouth as if that could save her. I hoped she'd bite it clean off.

Gradually, I realised everyone had left the room, so I gave up screaming and then my blood ran cold as I heard my dad say that he thought they might have to put me in a home. They would not dare. My mother, poor deluded woman, stuck up for me, but it was too late to change my mind about her. Mother told Dad that as I was their son, they had to cope and could not give up on me. The helper, a large ugly, stupid coarse woman, crossed herself and told my parents that some children were just born bad, and she said she had in all her life never cared for a child like me, so she was giving in her notice.

That night, after some sort of peace was established and my sister and I were in bed, me minus the restraints, my parents talked long and hard, and eventually, they decided to send my sister to my grandparents' home and my parents would try to devote more time to me to try and sort my behaviour out. Halleluiah, this was balm to my sore and bruised wrists and ankles, and I swore to myself that I would make them love me so much that they would not bring my hated sister back. What joy I waved my sister off with! I ignored the sorrow on the faces of my parents. At last, I had them to myself, better late than never.

CHAPTER 4

It worked, with my mother lavishing all her attention on me. I was well behaved, and I was happy. I choose to ignore the looks that my parents stole at me, and I refused to acknowledge the stiffness in their embraces. I had my parents and my home to myself. I loved to sit on my mother's knee. I cuddled and caressed her and sucked my thumb as she read stories or sang to me. How happy I was! I reasoned that I should have been an only child. I loved the attention I was getting even though I clearly saw how unhappy my parents were about the situation. I did not care. I hoped never to see my sister again. What did it matter to me if they were unhappy, as long as I was happy? So what? One day, I caught my mother holding a picture of my sister, and she was weeping, so I knew it was only a matter of time and sister would be back.

The day my sister came home, my frowns came back. My grandmother, a nosy old smelly woman, who I knew did not care for me, told my mother that it was unnatural for a family to be separated and that my parents had to be firm with me and stick no nonsense. My dad lifted me on to his knee, and he told me in no uncertain terms that it was my choice to, either behave and live with my family or my family would have no choice but to send me back.

Back? What was he talking about? I only found out years later, and by then, it was too late, much too late for them all.

I played by myself most of the time, and I ignored my sister. This behaviour endeared me to my mother, who was so relieved to be living in a somewhat normal home that she tried to give me most of her attention. It still wasn't enough for me, and I planned my offensive and my battles well. My war was far from over; the hostilities had just abated for a while. I was learning and honing my skills.

One fine day, we had a picnic. I really did enjoy myself, and I felt myself smile. It was such a rare thing for me to do because I had a permanent frown. I noticed my dad relax as he looked at me. I knew he was constantly watching me, and when he was at work, my mother kept my sister close by her at all times. I realised that they did not trust me to be alone with my sister, so I had to be crafty. I started to smile a lot, and I even laughed out loud one day, which shocked everyone to silence. Our home became, for the first time in my life, normal, but it was the calm before the storm, and I was the only one to know this, mainly because it was my raging storm that I held in check until the elements were right. My sister glimpsed the venom in my eyes, but I kept it hooded from my parents. I stayed away from sister, and when I felt I could not control my urges, I sought out the neighbourhood pets. They were insufficient for my needs but had to satisfy. I was biding my time; it would come. It would come in a blaze of glory, and it had to come soon, for I was struggling with pretence.

CHAPTER 5

School, and just what can I say about school that could be of use? I hated school. It was the first time I came across bigger and smarter bullies than myself, and, boy, how I suffered at their hands! But I persevered, and soon they recognised the bad in me and gave me my rightful place in their gang. I was soon at the top of the pecking order but learned a sharp lesson in keeping my actives well away from the teachers' prying eyes. I learned to be more deceitful, crueller, angrier, and even more devious, so school taught me something.

I had lots of little girls to practise on, but my sister was the one whom I lavished my attention on. How she suffered, and I sacrificed her up to the trials and tortures of my gang. Mother kept her at home, and that was the end of me torturing my sister at school. I still persecuted my sister at home, but the thought of her home alone with my mother made me protect her from all the bullies at school. Mother thought me so brave to stand up for my sister, deluded woman.

It was our sixth birthday, and my sister and I asked for a paddling pool. It was a great big pool with rigid sides, and it took my dad hours to erect and fill with water. Mother gave us new bathing costumes, and she went off to answer the door to our friends, the first friends we had ever invited to our home because our home had never been the type of home to invite people to. I, as usual, got the blame. It was never said, but I knew it was felt. How happy my parents looked! How sad I had to be the one to wipe the smiles off their faces!

I knew as I looked at my sister standing in her bright pink swimming costume that my rage was going to be hard to control, but when she laughed at my stupid black swimming shorts, my mind started to bend and melt just like a toffee does in your mouth as you chew it. She stood in front of the full-length mirror in our parents' bedroom, and she pirouetted round and round and lifted her arms above her head. Her soft blond curls bounced about her shoulders, and I could imagine the admiring looks and hear the compliments that our friends would give her.

I tore off my shorts, and I demanded she give me her suit. She laughed and had the audacity to say my winky was so small that I looked like her sister and if I put her suit on, everyone would mistake me for her. I realised at that moment that I wanted to be her. If I were her with my bright blond curls, my parents would love me to bits, and they could dress me up in pretty clothes. She had to go, so I calmly opened the window, and I heard the excited voices of children. I looked out to see loads of people arriving at our house, and I turned to my sister told her to look out at the presents they had brought for us. How quickly and eagerly she went to her death and how lovely she looked as she fell through the air with her blonde curls fanning out behind her like a veil but how shocked I was to see my dad standing in the doorway when I turned around! What had he seen? I never knew, and I don't think he knew either.

I remember the anguished look on his face and the desperate look in my mum's eyes that did not go away until it was replaced by a different look entirely.

There was no party after that. There was never a party after that. I remember the screams and the cries of parents and children, and I revelled in the attention I received from everyone. Everyone wanted to kiss me, but no one wanted to kiss my sister. How I loved it! Did I feel regret or remorse? Yes, I wished I had done it sooner. Her blond hair did not look so good with blood all over it, and her pretty face . . . well, let's say only a mother could call it pretty now. My only regret, the swimming suit, it was ruined.

The police came and questioned everyone. I held my breath when they talked to my dad, but he just held his head in his hands and cried out, 'I'm sorry, love. I'm so sorry. Forgive me.' Only people had seen Dad with the paddling pool he might have gotten the blame with his histrionics, and I would have loved that. I wished with all my heart I had thought of it, but after all, I was only six years old. I would improve with age. Imagine my mother and I all alone, just the two of us, what fun we could have.

Then came the disgusting sounds of my mother sobbing her heart out when the funeral director prised my sister out of my mother's arms and took her broken body away. It nearly killed me to hear my mother cry out of her love for my sister. I hoped I would never see my sister again. I was an only child now. I knew it would take some time for my mother to forget my sister. I had already, but I would be so loving that soon sister would fade to a memory, a memory that Mother would keep to herself. Halleluiah, my time had come.

Chapter 6

I remember how silent the house became when everyone left and how hard my mother held me to her breast. She kissed me over and over again, and I was in my glory. My dad had not spoken one word to me, and every time I glanced at him, he was looking at me with a strange and baleful stare. He told me to go to bed, but bless her, my mum took me upstairs and lay beside me until she thought I was sleeping. I refused to sleep; I knew my dad was up to something, so I needed to be ready with tears and sorrow if he accused me. What had he seen? He must be confused because he would have accused me by now. The wait was unbearable for me, but I refused to sleep.

He did accuse me, which made mother scream out, and she screamed so much the doctor was sent for. *My* mother was not to be calmed, and she hurled abuse at my dad when he told our doctor what he thought he had seen. Ah, he was confused, he had not actually seen me push my sister, but he knew me. Now, our doctor was a devious and unessential man, and I had come to blows with him on numerous occasions in the past. He also knew me for what I was, right from the start, and he wanted to believe my dad. I listened at the door to hear my mum scream that she did not want to lose both her children at once, for if she did, she would kill herself.

The gist of the plan my treacherous dad and our scheming doctor had thought up was to put me under the care of a physiatrist, residential, no less. I was to be incarcerated in a mental institute.

I pleaded, and I am ashamed to have to admit it, but I begged to be allowed to stay with my mother. I fell to the floor before my mother's chair, and I grabbed her legs and screeched that I would die in the hospital if they took me away from her. Where was my celebration at my sister's death, my going on outings alone with my mother, baking, reading, gardening? I beseeched my mother, to no avail. She let me down; she sat in that cursed chair and watched as they dragged me away. I know she was crying, but come on, she should have said no! They would not have dared take me without her consent. She should have shouted, threatened. She should have taken hold of me, wrapped me in her arms, and not let me go. No, she sat in that chair and watched as they tore me away from her legs, and she let them take me away from her. She is finished.

I don't remember going to the hospital, but I remember waking up there. I was so angry that I wanted to rip the place to shreds, but I talked to myself and made myself calm down and study my options. I knew I was too young to be legally held here, so I reasoned that my dad and our doctor had done a deal with the physiatrist so I had to outsmart them. What I really wanted to do was pull their sanctimonious heads off. Did they think I did not know what they were about? They wanted me to admit my crime. They wanted grief, remorse, repentance. What they got was me. Outsmart them, I did. I actually surprised myself because I was such a normal pleasant boy who answered all their twisted questions so beautifully that I was at home within a month. They probably thought my dad was as mad as a hatter and our doctor with him. Ha, ha! I would lock them up for their ineptitude.

I had missed my sister's funeral, but I was glad to. Why would I want to see all the attention that people would shower on her even in death? I could forgo all the hugs and sympathy that I knew I would receive rather than hear my sister called a beautiful angel and see her lying in a white padded coffin surrounded by flowers. I could close my eyes and just picture it with disgust. I was an only child now. How wonderful!

My home had disappeared in my absence. Where had my loving mother gone to be replaced with this lacklustre, sad, and empty vessel?

She tried, but her beloved was gone. She was suffering, and worse still, I could not cure her. I was so very good. I tried and I tried to bring a smile to her face, but all I received for my efforts was a sad lift of her lips. I lost count of the times I discovered her in Sister's bedroom. I thought of burning our house to the ground.

I was distraught. I had imagined and yearned in the hospital for my home life, my life with my parents as an only child, but my sister was still here in the midst of us and I became crazed with jealousy. If my parents mentioned her, I would throw a tantrum. My mum told my dad that it was my way of dealing with the pain of losing her, but my dad knew, and I knew he knew by the look he threw on me and by the way he started to avoid me.

CHAPTER 7

I confided to my mother that Dad believed I had pushed my sister but in fact I had tried to save her but I could not get a good enough grip on her swimsuit. I had achieved something; my mother turned against my dad because he stood by his belief that I had had something to do with my sister's death. Mother felt sorry for me, and, boy, did I exploit this. First, I had nightmares and had to be taken into my parents' bed. I lay sobbing in my mother's arms as she stroked me and crooned to me, but my dad got up and slept on the settee until this became a routine every night. Dad complained and put his foot down. Mother won, and I stayed in her bed while Dad moved into the spare room. How I loved to snuggle against her softness! Happiness was within my grasp, but I hated how she cried herself to sleep most nights, not because I was sorry for her heartache. Oh no, I knew she was thinking about my sister and that I could not have. That I would not allow. She had me now. Why did she cry for Sister? Could she not see how upset this was making me? I was furious.

One day, they made me visit my sister's grave and made me carry flowers to put on it. Were they mad? I was incensed to find it a shrine to her. They had put her body in the ground, but this . . . this was as if she lived, lived in this mound of brown earth. She was dust; she was nothing, as if she had never been born. What was this? They had put her teddy bear in a glass case on top of her grave. How morbid! Then I realised it was my teddy. They had got it wrong, stupid, stupid, people. A feeling of hatred and rage filled me so violently that I grabbed the glass case and smashed it to bits, then as I beheld my father's fury, I held my breath and I passed out. Poor bewildered mother thought it my grief, but my dad, well, he was wrong as well, he thought it guilt, but I had had enough. I was prepared for flowers but teddies, toys . . . she was dead, forget her, I had.

When we arrived home, Mother put me to bed, and dad and she sat in the garden, talking about my sister as they studied her face in the photo albums. I was sitting on the stairs listening. How could we move on and wipe her from our lives with all these constant reminders of her, so I took all the pictures off the walls, and, boy, were there lots of them and I calmly opened each frame and cut my sister out of them all. It took me ages, and I was delighted with my work. Pity I can't say the same for my dad. It took him a few hours to notice, and how I giggled at the look of pure horror on his ugly face! Then he thrashed me so badly that Mum intervened and told him to leave.

I was over the moon. I wish I had thought of it sooner. The severe beating was worth it. Happy, happy days, just the two of us, the way it should have always been. Dad returned. Mother had written to him behind my back, and she would pay for this lapse later. She missed him . . . missed him. How dare she not be satisfied with me, me who had gone to so much trouble so that we could be alone. Life, with mother and I, was never the same, and daily, Dad seemed to shrink before our eyes. He came home late and left early. He rarely ate with us, and when he did, it was as if the food was choking him. Mother saw the looks he bestowed on me, and she became cold towards him. How thrilled I was when she refused to allow him to remove me from her bed. She told him I needed her, I was suffering, I was unhappy, I was delirious, and I was in my element. We hardly spoke to him, my mother and I. We needed no one, least of all him. One day, he just left, and I never saw him again. Can't honestly say I was sorry. I discovered that he had taken all the pictures of my sister out of our albums and left any with me in them behind. It saved me getting rid of them, but it hurt my mother so much. I think she was glad Dad had left. She never mentioned him again. Well, why would she? She had me, hadn't she? Now, we were complete.

CHAPTER 8

My mother and I, has a certain ring to it, but I thought I would be happy, and I wasn't. My mother was not the same woman. She had shrunk, she looked bewildered most of the time, and she had nothing to offer me, nothing but boredom, plus she had to work because my delightful dad had disappeared and we had no money. I was left alone much of the time, so I kept to myself, and I found I had a flair for computers, so I spent every waking moment increasing my knowledge to the extent that I was what is referred to as a wiz kid in my chosen profession. Yes, it is my profession. Killing is my hobby.

When I was ten and again when I was fourteen and when I was sixteen, my mother tried to get me out of her bed, but she was mine, and I enjoyed her. I wish I could say she enjoyed our special times. Did I care? Nah! Who needed the silly girls I was in school with. They all reminded me of my fat sister, especially the blond ones. I never missed an opportunity to pinch and abuse them when no one was around to see. I used to ambush them when they asked to go to the toilets. I had them so threatened with extreme violence that they rarely told on me. I used to do all the guys' homework so they thought me great, and because I charmed the teachers, the girls knew no one would believe them. Ricky . . . Ricky is such a nice guy. I was a nice guy because I needed a cloak of niceness to hide my actions behind.

One girl, a really feisty blond, thought she would stand up to me. What a mistake! I followed her for weeks until I knew every step she took, and then I pounced. She was my first rape, and she was great. I will never forget my first time, and neither will she, but for very different reasons. I never left a mark on her that was visible, but she could not walk properly for ages. I used to mimic her walk. Why did she not tell? I left her in no uncertainty what would happen to her if she did. I spread so many disgusting rumours about what she had done with me that she left school because of the jeers and taunts from the boys. Years later, I read she had jumped from the school roof, nothing to do with me. I heard rumours that she was a prostitute and took drugs, such a pretty face smashed to pulp on the concrete. I no more pushed her than I pushed my sister.

What could Mother do? I was all she had, but she shrank before my eyes and became so ugly that I raged at her and accused her of doing it on purpose. How could my sister and I have been so pretty and our parents so ugly I demanded to know, so she told me and everything that had gone before, fell into place. That is when I knew I did not want her anymore.

CHAPTER 9

Back, I remember my dad saying I had to go back, and I laughed at the idea of me going back into my mother's womb. But that is not what he meant at all, and how could I have misunderstood? I misunderstood because the horror was too much for me. I was adopted. My parents thought they could not have children, and they applied to adopt me. Me, an unwanted and unloved baby still in my treacherous birth mother's tummy, they paid for me. Why my birth mother had not just got rid of me, I don't know. I refuse to try to make excuses for her and her situation. She could have kept me instead of selling me, and she did sell me even though Mother tries to make excuses for her and says that they only gave her enough money for her medical expenses.

My parents then discovered that mother was pregnant and rather than let someone else have me, they agreed to take me and pretend that my sister, who was actually born three weeks after me, was my twin. So you see everything that came after was their fault. With their lies and deceit, they had caused it all. If they had not been so greedy, I would have been with a family that loved me, an only child maybe and not living in a family that had me because they were sorry for me. What I would have achieved had they left me to be adopted by others, people who would see my potential and have only me and give me all their love? Guess whose actual birthday we celebrated?

I looked at this stupid woman who had just murdered me, and I was filled with contempt and hatred. They were reaping what they had sowed; a million heartaches blossomed from the lies and deceit they had planted. I was planted in arid soil mixed in with weeds when my seed should have been cultivated in a hot house. I would have bloomed in splendour, not choked before I flowered. I had loved this woman, but she had betrayed me, so I fetched her a drink and I handed her huge boxes of paracetamol and I told her about how I had pushed my sister out of the window. She was speechless. I left nothing out. All my misdemeanours I laid at her pathetic feet, and I felt fascinated watching her digesting this information and thrilled at the horror in her eyes. I informed my mother that it was all her fault because she had never loved me enough and now I knew the reason. Had I not always felt different? My feelings were shot to pieces. I was not her natural child. I was an unwelcome intrusion into their cosy lives. This was the reason she had always put my sister before me. 'Why,' I screamed at her, 'when I have spent my whole life trying to make you love me?' My love was not a son's love, and I knew this, but now, I could understand why I felt this way about her. I was not her natural son. I screamed my anger and rage out until I was hoarse, and I told her I hoped she rotted in hell for the hurt she had caused me. I screamed that she should take the tablets and die because she was no use to me anymore. How could I love her after all these lies? Just die and go away.

My mother looked at me with tears in her eyes, and she told me, the liar, that she did love me. She told me she had loved me the second I was handed to her after I was born, and she tried to tell me that she loved me as much as she had loved my sister and she understood how I felt. How on earth could she understand how I felt? She said she felt so sorry for me. The bitch, I don't want her sympathy. I wanted her love. My mother swallowed all the tablets, and she said once more that she loved me, and she closed her eyes and lay down on the sofa.

I watched her die, a slow but peaceful death, and I felt relief as I looked at this woman who had presumed to call herself my mother, this pathetic bag of bones had had the audacity to believe that she could mother me. She was a failure as a wife and as a mother. I studied her as she breathed her last shallow breaths. I watched as her lips turned blue, how had I ever touched such as she never mind loved her, now she disgusted every fibre of my being. When all was said and done she was an ugly bitch. I really have given her a taste of the Ricky magic. This did nothing for me, this painless death, but she was so ugly that I could not touch her.

Was I curious about my real mother? Did I wish to find her? Not on your life. I hated her more than I hated this one before me. Actually, I more than hated her. I did not acknowledge her; she did not exist. I had been abandoned by two women, me, but I did not need them. I would show them that I, Ricky, could live without them. What goes around, ladies, comes around. One mother had got her just desserts; the other, her price was in never knowing me.

Now, I had closure, and my life could begin, so I closed the door behind me, closed the door on this rotten house filled with unfulfilled dreams, and I walked out. Whoever liked could dispose of the wreck of a woman I had left behind. I was ready, more than ready. I had a bad taste in my mouth, and I needed sweet lips to kiss me better.

CHAPTER 10

The first time was so exquisite. I relived it over and over again, and she was so very pretty, blond curly hair tumbling down her back. I planned nothing, but they fell into my lap. They asked for it, these silly young girls, out on their own far too late at night and without an older brother for protection. They were a wonderful interlude to my life along with my serious computer work. I found myself in great demand all over the country, and my favourite places to work, the police stations. I loved to set up their profiles of serial killers, and I laughed at their feeble attempts to understand the mind of a killer. How I laughed at their sad and stupid attempts to understand the mind of a genius! They didn't have a clue. We had nothing to fear from these dopes, and really all they had to do was ask me.

They would never ask me. I was too clever for this lot. I was Ricky, the nice guy who fixed their computers. The nice quiet guy who blended into the background with his unassuming ways so that every snippet of information the police acquired about murders, the nice guy heard. Most of it did not interest me. Well, you know the reason for that, but the information I learned about my victims' home life thrilled me to bits and fed my hunger for more.

Lonely, I could hardly believe it, but I missed having someone to come home to. I decided that instead of getting rid of one of the girls after two days, I would bring her home, but where could I keep her? My mind is delightfully inventive, so I designed my special bed, and I even surprised myself with the results. It was time for a new start, so I bought a nice house in a very quiet neighbourhood. My guest room, gym, was ready and waiting, and I could barely contain myself.

What luck I have, only a few months in my new home and I have my partner! An older woman, but she will suffice. I could not believe my luck when I saw Rina standing on her doorstep gazing at the stars. Stars, the last thing she saw in freedom. Boy, but she was heavy, and how glad I was that it was two in the morning and everyone was asleep! It took me about an hour to trail her across the grass and up into the guest bedroom, her bedroom where she and I would have some good times in the future. How easily and perfectly she fitted on to the ingenious contraption I had designed for her, made for me by an unsuspecting mechanic who thought I worked in the movies. I congratulated myself so much I was practically lightheaded. How smoothly she fitted into the bed, and I thanked the French for inventing such deep beds. This is what I had been born for. This would be my finest hour. If and when I could not grab a girl, I would always have Rina waiting for me at home. I made a bet with myself how long I could keep her, and after my first experience of her, I reckoned, if I restrained myself, I might manage to keep her alive for two years.

Two years and then, well, it all depends on how I feel at the time. What a family she has! They are worse than mine, pretending to be close and loving when in reality the husband has a mistress and the daughter and son are spoilt and love themselves. I do so enjoy befriending them and taking information back to Rina, so she knows just how much they don't miss her.

I see I have a project in the son. He is the one to miss his mum, but I know I can step into the breach she has left. I wonder how long it will take me to supplant her. They are my new family, and I am growing quite fond of them all.

Tom, how easy you are! You have no substance, no strength of character. How can you not smell your mother off me when I have come straight from her to you? Instead, you surround yourself with her clothes and cover your skin with her perfume until you stink. Why have you not found her? Why have you not sought her out? Because you just miss your clothes washed and ironed and your meals made. You miss a mother for the work she does for you, not for herself. I sound like I care, but I don't. I like to see them flounder, and I revel in delight when they fall apart and begin to implode.

I love to spend time in their family and then I absolutely love to go home and spend quality time with my Rina, regaling her with tales of her former family. They did not know what they had.

I can't believe how easy this has all been. The police are twats, and I have heard them talk when I bring food to Rina's house. They think Rina has gone off with someone because she found out about Steve's girlfriend. They are so bad at looking for her that I reckon Rina will never be found, dead or alive. The police are hopeless. I have left them no clues, but I reckon if I left my name and address, they would get the street wrong. Where did they think a woman who had taken nothing with her go to? How very easy to leave them no clues, but I wish I had not closed the door that night. I wish I had left it wide open and then it would be more interesting for me and more exciting, but at the moment, it feels like taking a bone from a toothless dog.

The girls seem to queue up for me to take them, but they are mostly weak and it is over too soon and the whole messy scene leaves me unsatisfied. I want them to fight me, and I want them to make me feel alive. I am happier spending time with Rina even though she is starting to age. She is far too skinny, and her body has no substance to it. Maybe, she needs exercise. I will sort that out.

My life has meaning now, and I am sublimely happy. Everything has fallen into place for me. I have a great and interesting job. I have a woman whom I can enjoy any time, and she is up for anything. Tom and I are a couple. I seduced him on his sister's wedding day. I even let Rina stay out of her bed, and I kindly left her at the window so that she could watch her daughter not miss her mother on her wedding day. It has turned out one of the best days of my life. I seduced Tom in the next bedroom where Rina lived, and I knew she could hear me having sex with her son. It felt like a threesome for me. Tom dotes on me, and even though he still talks on and on about his mum, I encourage this because it gives me a thrill finding out things I can torture Rina with. My strategy would have been more accomplished if Rina's abduction had not been so spur of the moment, opportunistic profilers call it. I think I could have had all the family in my web. This is my new and delightful design. The next time, I will plan it better. I am elated with myself and so proud of what I have accomplished.

I am so annoyed with Rina. She thinks she has won, but she has no idea how bad it can get. I thought she would be glad to smell Tom off me when I went to her after Tom had left, but oh no, she pretended not to hear me. She is lucky to be alive. She drove me to such violence that spoiled the lovely glow I was experiencing. I will not lose my family now. I am not near ready yet. I am nowhere near finished. In actual fact, I am only beginning.

RINA

CHAPTER 1

The woman in the mirror beckons me, and as I look in her eyes, memories flood my mind, and I close my eyes and let my life flow before me in rich technicolour splendour. Susan, you may have taken my place, but you can't take my memories, memories so precious of my son and my daughter and I luxuriate in the movie that plays before me, so enrapt that I don't even notice that I am back in my dark place.

I feel I have lived here forever and I have accepted that I will not be found, not in the way I want to be anyway. I have fantasised about my rescue over and over again until, some days, I wake up and I am shocked that I am still in my coffin. I can't believe how fast the time seems to fly by, and yet it drags by also. He still uses me when he has not the opportunity to abduct another victim. Part of me is glad to think that when he is with me, he is not torturing some terrified little girl. He is not particular, and my heart has bled for his victims when he whispered of his adventures while he abused me. I thought of their poor destroyed families, and I wondered how they would ever recover or how they would live with their agony.

My vigil at the window continues. It is amazing how much I know about my family's lives from watching them come and go each day. I have given up pleading with them to look up because I know they couldn't see me even if they did. I know without him telling me that the window is not an ordinary one. I marvel at how big Tom has grown, and I never get enough of watching him shoot balls in our drive. My heart bursts with pride when I see Lucy. She has grown into a fine young woman and seems so in love with this tall stranger. I hate it when I see Steve with Susan, and I plan the revenge I will take on this pair. The day Steve carried Susan over my, my threshold, was excruciatingly painful. I was so full of hurt that even the pain the animal inflicted on me failed to make me cry. I felt my eyes blazing with fury and defiance.

I paid for my show of defiance. I was still fed the smoothies, and I was still washed, but he had begun to let me walk around the room, for exercise as he termed it. I can only guess that it was part of his torture regime. One day, I tried to make a run for the door, but he broke both my ankles, so I dragged myself across the floor, and he broke my wrists. Then I rolled across the floor, and he kicked me so many times that I passed out.

CHAPTER 2

I am hungry, and I am dirty. I never in my wildest dreams thought I would look forward to him coming for me, but I am. I crave the first taste of my smoothie. When had I grown to enjoy them? Where is he? I am bewildered and confused, disoriented, and terrified. I can hardly breathe, and I fear I am going to drown in the fog of my own bodily wastes.

What has happened to this jailer of mine to turn him into a creature so vile and sadistic? He eventually lifted me out of my box, and he beat me hard because of the state I was in. He rushed me through the shower, hardly rinsing the lavender off so that I was stinging all over. He forgot to feed me, and he seemed preoccupied. Soon, I would know why he was distracted.

I heard the noises they made. I was meant to. My beautiful young son, how can I bear this sacrilege? How my heart lifted and sang with hope when I first heard your voice and I thought you had come for me. I could almost feel your arms about me, and I yearned for your breath upon my face. An abyss opened before me when I realised what my monster had planned for us. I prayed like I have never prayed before that God would not let this creature harm you and constrain you in a contraption like mine. I bargained with God that I would gladly give my life so that my son could live. I heard my son talk to this excuse of a man. I heard him call the monster, Ricky, heard him call his name in pleasure — Ricky, an ordinary name, for a most evil man. I heard him talk about me, and I felt the pain in his voice, pain that made me cry for love, and I listened to my tormentor telling my son to let go of his love for me and transfer it to him, his lover. My darling son is seduced while his mum is held captive in the adjoining room. May he never find out. God, please help me find a way out of this heartache, for I can take no more of this.

I heard the door shut, and I heard his footsteps as he came for me. I knew his evil desires, and my mind could not take this last inequity, so I fell into the blessed pit and felt no more. At last, I am free.

CHAPTER 3

Blank, empty, gone, space, voices, voices. Whose voices are they? Tears? I am not crying. Whose tears are falling on my face? Who is crying, gulping the tears down and swearing, swearing? I walk through the valley of the shadow of death. Finally, I am dead, but God has promised there will be no tears in heaven or pain, but the pain is still here. It lives in me. I will fear no evil, but I fear. I tried but I did not succeed. I am terrified of him. Thy rod and thy staff, please comfort me and rescue me from the presence of mine enemies and prepare a place for me in the Lord's house forever. For your old life has gone and there will be no more suffering, neither will there be any more pain. Revelation.

'Rina, Rina, we have got you out. Rina can you hear me? Rina you are safe!'

Mum, is it you, Mum? No, Rina, you are the mum now. No, I don't want to be a mum. I don't want children. Lucy, Tom, I can't save them. I want to be a little girl curled up on your knee. Rina, you have two children. No, I don't want them. I can't be responsible for them. I want to be a little girl. I want you to protect me. Ricky will get Lucy and Tom, so if I never grow up, I can't have children. If I have any children, the monster will get them. He will do unspeakable things to them and devour them. If I never have children, then he cannot get them. He, Ricky, cannot harm them. They will be safe if they are never born.

Let the little children come unto me. I will bring you to the living water. Let me lie down in this warm water. Let it clean my body and soul and scrub my skin, until all trace of him is obliterated. Let me lie down on sheets as soft as babies' skin, and let me sleep in the Lord's house forever. My cup runneth over. Surely, goodness and mercy will follow me all the days of my life. Please let me live in this house, this cotton wool house forever.

He has replaced the bulb. No, it is a new light, and it shines so bright. He has covered me with a sheet, and I am in a bed. Where is he? What has he planned for me now? I don't care. I am beyond caring. Suffer the little children, what children. My children . . . are they suffering? There will be no more suffering. Behold, all things are made new. All things, even me? Am I made new? I hope so for the old me is damaged beyond measure. I will get a new body because the old one is gone. There will be no more tears. No more sacrifices. The old way is gone. Behold, I have made all things new.

CHAPTER 4

Today, I moved my legs, just an inch, but I moved them, nonetheless. He has not fed me, but I don't feel hunger. I moved my arms, and I realised I was dreaming. I dreamt I was in a soft warm bed, covered by clean dry sheets so light they skimmed my flesh with gossamer sighs. My contraption was gone, and I was comfortable, and I had no more pain. I have to wake up, and I don't want to. I want to go on dreaming like this. I could live happily like this. I must be dreaming. I am dreaming a beautiful rainbow dream; the colours cascade around me and dance and dance inside my head. Pillows of fluffy clouds cuddle into my body, and I float along in a tunnel of soothing sweet music. I am in heaven, and I am happy to find myself dead and my mind fills with dreams of peace.

In my dream, his ugly vicious hands are tender as they touch my skin. In my dream, his evil face is solicitous, and his dead eyes are caressing me. I will not waken up. I refuse to waken. I prefer to stay in my dream.

In my dream, there are people to comfort me and keep me company. They talk softly to me and ask me questions. Can't they see I have a tape over my mouth, so I cannot answer their questions? I want to . . . I want to ask about my family. I want to ask about my son, for there is something so bad about my son that I try to remember but it stays on the horizon of my conscience and I can't grasp it. I feel so safe here. I pray my son is here also.

In my dream, they removed the tape from my mouth, but I can't open my mouth, and I don't think I can talk. But today, I saw them. Who are they and where is 'he'?

Where is he and where am I? It is night-time, and I open my eyes and I find myself in a small room, a small white room, without a window. I realise that I am in a hospital room. Is this a miracle, am I safe, was I found? Who is this large man sitting by my bed? He is sleeping, and I study him, but I don't know him. I don't recognise the dark slightly greying hair or the shape of his shoulders. Why is he sitting by my bed? More importantly, why is he holding my hand? I try to remove my hand without waking him, but suddenly, he lifts his head up, and when he registers that I am looking back at him, he jumps up and starts shouting. Please don't let my tormentor appear, please don't call him, don't, don't, please. I feel safe here. I don't want to go back to my darkness. I don't want to see his face again.

People appear; they are doctors and nurses, and they are crying but smiling also. The noise is deafening, but I can sense they are happy with me, and they all seem to talk at once. Someone raises my bed up, and I am looking at a mirror and I look for my friend, the old lady. I want to tell her I am safe and that I like this place and I am sorry but I will try not to return to my prison. My friend is there, but I see she has taken my advice. She has cut her hair, and even though it is still grey, it looks a lot better. She is not so skinny, but she is still very pale, and the horrible marks on her skin are not so noticeable, but her eyes . . . unfortunately, they are still dark with pain. She should come here, for she will be safe here. I like it here. I could stay here forever.

Who is this man sitting by my bed? I wish he would waken and explain a few things to me. I want to know where I am. I have an awareness of being free, but I am terrified that it is transience. Should I just enjoy this feeling of softness and not let the world and its people encroach on this exquisite cocoon I am floating in. I fall in and out of sleep, but every time I wake, my 'guardian angel' is beside my bed, and when I see his shape beside me, I relax and know I am safe.

I have been rescued. Halleluiah, I am free! I am me again, and I have survived. I have walked out of the darkness into the sunshine, so

I thank you, God, for answering my prayers. I try to sit up, and a bell sounds somewhere near. The man beside me stirs, sits up, and bestows a smile so gentle on me that it is my undoing and I start to howl. Howl is a good description, and I am horrified by the sound I am making. I try to say sorry, but only grunts come out. A feeling grows in my chest, and my heart expands so much I feel it will explode out of my body with relief.

The man raises my bed, and he tries to hold me, but at his touch, I open my mouth and a noise like nothing I have ever heard bangs off the walls. I realise I am cringing in my bed and the man beside me lays his head on the bed, and I hear him weeping. My room is soon full of doctors and nurses, and I let one nurse hold my hand, and looking at their faces, I see only concern. I realise that the man was only trying to comfort me. I am sorry, I have hurt him.

What has my jailer done to me? I will get over this feeling of terror. I am safe now, and I feel a determination start to form in me, a determination to recover. Where are my family? I long to see them and hold them in my arms.

I opened my eyes to find the man still sitting by my bed looking at me, and I panicked at first, then I relaxed and I tried to smile. I must have succeeded because he smiled back, and he began talking to me. What a kind and yet sad face with huge brown eyes full of regret! I knew I was safe with this man guarding me.

I have a journey to make, a long hard one. I want my family back, and I knew I could do it. We would be stronger because of this event, but we would survive.

MIKE

Chapter 1

I did not like this guy standing before me trying to explain to Montgomery about how his wife could be missing, for dear knows how long, and he does not notice. I had been a cop for too many years to accept that this was a normal family. Something was wrong. If he was not guilty of her disappearance, he was guilty of something, and I was determined to find out what. Some people can hide their guilt, but most people carry the burden of their sins about with them like a suitcase, and I reckoned that his suitcase was full.

He had the audacity to try and blame his lack of knowledge of his wife's disappearance on his wife. He kept going on and on about her always working at the crisis centre and how he never knew from one day to another where she would be. I did not think he had murdered her because he seemed genuinely worried about her, but I knew he was hiding something. He squirmed and pulled at his shirt collar a lot, a sure sign of his discomfort. It did not take us long to discover about his mistress, and when he asked that we not question her, I felt like smacking him in the face. He thought that his having a mistress was not relevant to the situation. How can he be so ignorant to believe that his having a mistress had nothing to do with the wife disappearing? Some men are twats, and I lost any sympathy I had felt for him. In fact, I know I gave him a hard time, but I could not help myself. This guy had gotten under my skin in a big way. Montgomery knew my past, and he guessed where the anger was coming from, so he gently tried to rein me in.

The son, him I could feel for, to lose a mum and then find out the dad you adored and looked up to had cheated on your mum was a lot to deal with. He was the only one in this sorry excuse of a family to blame himself for his mum's disappearance. The other two hurt my ears with their gripes about the way the mum had lived her life. I watched this young unhappy boy grow more and more desperate as the months dragged by. I think if he had had other relations, he would cope better, but he had no aunts or uncles or even grandparents to talk to, and as his dad got on with living with his girlfriend and his sister became more and more wrapped up in her boyfriend, he was sadly on his own. My heart broke to see him flounder, and I vowed to keep an eye on him. I was glad to see him befriended by the neighbour even though the neighbour was far too old for him. At least, I reasoned with myself, he has someone.

This was one of those cases that every cop hates. A total mystery, no clues, no evidence, in fact nothing. It was as if Rina Scott had fallen off the face of the earth or had never existed at all. I really thought she had found out about her husband's infidelity and hoofed it, but she had literally taken nothing with her, absolutely nothing. There was nothing more we could do after we had put posters up, made a TV request, and questioned everyone who lived in the town. We were beaten and no closer to discovering what had happened to her, and I know the general consensus was the same as my own, that she had just left.

Her son, Tom, made me promise not to give up on his mum, and after seeing him wander the streets looking for her, I decided to keep an open mind and not write her off. I met the neighbour, and I disliked him instantly. I did not think his friendship with Tom was healthy, but in view of the fact that Tom had no one else to turn to, his dad wrapped up in his own occupations and totally ignoring his son, I felt I could not intervene. I tried to rationalise this dislike for Ricky because he was very good to the family. He spent a fortune feeding them, but he just annoyed the hell out of me. I decided to keep in touch with this family just to see that the boy could cope, or maybe because I had lost my own son, I felt badly for this boy, and I wished the dad would wake up before he lost him forever. I guessed that with work, their relationship would mend, but the dad seemed oblivious to the boy's pain, or maybe he just didn't care. I cared more than I wanted to, so I dropped in every few weeks and then every few months as the time went by, but I always left feeling depressed, sorry for the son and even sorrier for the missing mum because life went on in that house as if she had never existed.

CHAPTER 2

I read about the girl's wedding in the local paper, and I dropped by the church. I was dismayed to see how ill young Tom looked. He not only looked ill, but I could see he was also shaking with ill concealed anger, and I realised how hard this must be for him. As for the rest of the family, they just looked like any other family, and I marvelled at how quickly the dad and daughter had accepted the disappearance of the mum. From all accounts, the mum had been a good mother and a faithful wife, so I found their actions hard to stomach. Profoundly, I felt Tom was on his own in his grief, so I decided to give him some support, but Ricky had beaten me to it. I left the church with a feeling of disquiet. Why? I wasn't sure, but I did not like the way Ricky looked at the boy. I had a bad feeling at the pit of my stomach, and I decided to pay Tom a visit.

CHAPTER 3

Later that week, I arrived at Rina's house. Tom seemed pleased to see me, and I noticed at once the change in him. He was happy, and gone was the haunted and deranged look in his eyes. He talked non-stop about Ricky, and at once, I felt ashamed and guilty of the thoughts I'd had about this man who had been the only friend this young boy had had. I realised he was in love with Ricky, and he was really happy, so I was somewhat relieved.

My relief was short-lived when Ricky appeared, and the feelings I had had before of him reappeared. I just could not get away from the disquiet I felt, and I did not like the way he sized me up. Tom was oblivious to the tension in the air, and he chatted away. I decided to keep in touch with Tom because I still did not trust this Ricky. My gut feeling was that he was not as genuine as he pretended.

As I was leaving, I noticed something lying on the grass by the side of the house, and when I walked towards it, I saw it was a dead cat. I looked to see what could have happened to it, and I found the way it was lying on the ground peculiar. Cats always land on their paws, and this one was no exception, but the force the cat had hit the ground with had broken all four legs, so I reckoned this particular cat had not fallen but been thrown from a distance. I looked over at the nearest house, Ricky's house, and my gaze was drawn up to a window in the side of the house. As the sun shone on it, it too looked peculiar. I chided myself for my imagination, but I picked the cat up and returned to the house.

Chapter 4

Tom was distraught and informed me the cat belonged to his mum. Rina's cat? When I told him where I had found the cat, he told me he was fed up trying to keep the cat out of Ricky's garden because Ricky was allergic to cats and hated them. Tom told me of the rows Ricky and he had had over this cat and then he turned to Ricky and said, 'I suppose you are glad now she is dead, but she always reminded me of the day my mum disappeared. She only sat in the side garden. She didn't cause any trouble. I don't understand why you hated her so much Ricky?'

I felt the hairs on my neck stand up, and a peculiar sensation formed in the pit of my stomach, the same sensation I get when I am called out to a crime. I suddenly knew why the cat sat in the side garden, and as I looked in Ricky's eyes, I knew he was suspicious of what I was thinking. I hoped I had been trained well, and I hoped I had acted normal when I was feeling anything but . . .

I said I was sorry about the cat, and I left, but I drove around the corner and sat in the car, pretending to phone while I worked out what actions I should take. Was I just full of imagination? Was my mind out of control and seeing things that were not there? No, my gut told me otherwise. I knew I was right. Now, what was I to do? I knew I could not make a mistake, not this time.

I eventually phoned Montgomery. I told him about my suspicions, and after a tense discussion and a few threats, from both of us, he thankfully trusted my intuition, and soon, a police car roared into the street and up to Tom's drive. It roared to a stop, and Montgomery stepped out. I followed on foot, and I was amazed at the way Montgomery informed Ricky that he was under arrest for the murder of the cat, and I nearly laughed at the look on Ricky's face when Montgomery handcuffed him.

The threats and the curses came fast and furious, and when Ricky realised that Montgomery was taking him to the police station and I was staying behind, he knew I knew, and the evil that distorted his face shocked me to the core and confirmed to me that he had something to do with Rina's disappearance.

Tom was aghast and pleaded with me to let Ricky go because he had been joking about the cat. He told me Ricky would not hurt a fly and that he, Tom, loved him and he asked to go with Ricky in the police car. I needed Tom out of the way, in case I was correct in my suspicions, so I agreed.

Chapter 5

I knew I should wait on the warrant that was on its way, but I couldn't wait. My senses told me to hurry, but my legs were like jelly as I crossed the garden towards Ricky's house, worrying about what I might find. I looked up at the side window, and I knew where my search would begin.

My legs started working, and I kicked and kicked the kitchen door until it gave way. I ran in with my heart hammering in my chest, my blood racing. I took the stairs two at a time, and I soon worked out the room I wanted.

It was bare of furniture except for a large wooden French-style bed and Ricky's treadmill. I checked all the walls, but they were smoothly plastered and painted, and except for the amount of mirrors, nothing showed up to signify a concealed cupboard. I knocked every inch of wall to see if there could be any space hidden. I checked behind each mirror thinking how conceited this guy is to want to see himself as he works out. How strange! The ceiling was intact as well, so I checked the bathroom. Except for the nauseating smell of lavender, it looked like any other bathroom except that this one was ultra-clean. This made me even more suspicious.

The rest of the bedrooms were just bedrooms, sparse but beautifully decorated. My next thought was the roof space. Nothing, there was nothing in the roof space except a string of Christmas lights and a child's Christmas stocking. I knew all this was odd, but maybe, I was wrong in my assumptions about Rina, and I felt despondent.

Again, I thoroughly checked every room, the walls, the ceilings, and even the doors. I opened every cupboard in the whole house, but they were all empty. All this emptiness just confirmed to me that we were dealing with a strange and maybe dangerous man. He must have bought the food he gave to the neighbours. All I could find in the fridge were smoothies, dozens of packets, smoothies filled with loads of nutrients. These were for Rina. I knew it. The bastard was keeping her alive with this disgusting stuff.

I knew I was quickly running out of time. I knew Montgomery could not hold Ricky much longer, and I knew if Ricky got a lawyer, he would walk in minutes. I fought to get my thoughts under control. I just knew she was in that room somewhere. I could feel her presence, feel her desperation, even feel her pain. The walls vibrated with it, but why could I not find her?

When I stood at the window and looked across at Rina's house, the oppressive feeling I experienced confirmed that I was right and she was in this room, this sickening room that smelt of lavender and something else—death. I could smell death.

I sat down on the bed, and I put my head in my hands, and I noticed hairs stuck to the bed, but they were cat's hairs. The cat, she had to be here. The cat knew it, and now so did I. Rina, I'm here, can you hear me? Suddenly, it came to me, she was under the floorboards. How stupid of me! That is where I should have looked first. With hope flaring in me, I pushed and shoved the large heavy bed to one side.

A feeling of total despair engulfed me when I realised that the floor was intact, and I fell, to my knees, distraught. I knew that if I did not find her, he would be back, and if she was still alive, he would kill her and dispose of her body and that would be the end of Rina. We would never know what had happened to her, and I was convinced that she lived. I felt it in my heart, or I hoped it in my soul.

CHAPTER 6

Fury filled my body as I ran back down the stairs, two, three at a time and out into the garden, but the garden was as strange as the house. It had no garden sheds; it did not even have a garage. There was nowhere to hide a body. I frantically searched the garden itself, but nothing jumped up at me to show where a body might be hidden or buried.

Hopelessly, I looked up at the window again, and my heart told me she was in that room. Where? So I raced back up the stairs and into the room, but it was useless. I knew there was nothing more I could do apart from demolishing the house, and I was filled with a violent anger that burst out of me and I took my rage and frustrations out on the bed. Screaming and shouting abuse, I tore at the mattress and coverings until my nails were bleeding and the sheets were in tatters. I threw the mattress to the floor, and I kicked the base of the bed. Suddenly, my rage dissipated, and I fell to my knees in despair. Then the red violent fog in my head cleared as I noticed a space between the cover and the base.

I can't remember what was going through my exhausted mind as I lifted the cover off the base, and I don't recall sinking to the floor and throwing up all over it, but I remember clearly my first glimpse of Rina. I knew it was her and not another woman, and I knew I was too late and the feeling of remorse scorched my heart. I closed my eyes and shook my head from side to side, and I made a promise to this tortured woman that I would make Ricky pay dearly. I would see that he suffered worse than she had, if I had to do it to him myself.

I phoned Montgomery, and I screamed at him down the phone, 'I have found her. I have found her. The bastard has killed her. Keep him there until I get there.' I phoned the mortuary and asked for a car, and I forced myself to look at this pitiful wreck of a woman. I will never forget the sight I looked upon. I thought in thirty years in the police, I had seen everything, but I had never encountered abuse on this scale.

She opened her eyes, and I was so shocked that I thought I had imagined it. I felt the hairs stand up at the back of my neck, and I tried to get some control over my emotions. I had to help her, so I felt for her pulse, and I jumped when I discovered that she had one. Quickly, I phoned for an ambulance, and stammering and stuttering, I screamed, 'She is alive. Get an ambulance here quickly.' I gently held her hand, a hand that brought fresh tears to my eyes. It was so smashed that it felt like a bag of bones that I held. With all my might, I willed her to hold on to whatever threads of life that she had left. I carefully removed the tape from her mouth, and she winced and again opened her eyes, and I fell back in horror at the dark vacant look in their depths. I wanted so much for her to live, but as I gazed at the empty blank pupils, I wondered if she was better off dying. How I wondered, could she recover from this trauma? The thought of her being here so close to her home left me tortured and I broke down and cried huge tears of remorse, tears that wracked my body but still tears that could not cleanse my guilt at not finding her sooner.

CHAPTER 7

I was still crying as I let the paramedics in the front door, but I was past caring what anyone thought of me. I saw the horror on their faces when they first beheld Rina, and I watched like a mother hen how they cared for her. I need not have worried for they were as gentle with her as they would have been with a baby, and they cried along with me at each mark they discovered. The paramedics decided to leave her on the contraption that she was strapped to, and I agreed with them because we did not know how badly she was injured and we were frightened of killing her before she was hospitalised. How slowly and carefully we carried our patient down the stairs. She might have been a corpse except her face was not covered by the beautiful but hateful covering off Ricky's bed.

Ordinarily, I would have marvelled at the intricate and well-designed contraption she was strapped to, but I was filled with such anger and hatred that I wanted to destroy this hideous thing as soon as I could. Thankfully, no nosy neighbours seemed to want to investigate the ambulance, and I was relieved to get her into the back of it, albeit across the top of the two ambulance beds. I phoned the hospital and requested they cordoned off an area where we could take her to. I did not want anyone seeing her in this state. The journey to the hospital was the longest of my life, but I talked to Rina and begged her not to let go. There was a glimmer of hope, and I clung to that with a tenacity that left my lips chewed and my limbs in a rigour as I willed Rina to live.

To the day I die, I will be grateful for the tender care the doctors and nurses lavished on Rina. Not one of them shirked from tending to her injuries, and the tears they shed on her arrival nearly drowned her. They had a mission to save her, and they pulled out all the stops. Once I knew she was in good hands, I left to confront her torturer. My limbs ached with the tension, but I knew as I drove to the police cell that I could not go near Ricky for I realised my anger would push me to go for him, I would not be able to control myself, and I knew I would kill him if I saw him, so I went looking for Montgomery.

CHAPTER 8

I was taken aback by the sight of Montgomery. He was drinking, a whiskey no less, and suddenly, I noticed his pale face, untidy hair, and unMontgomery-like appearance. I raised my eyes. He shook his head from side to side and told me Ricky was dead, shot by a new rookie who had panicked when Ricky made a lunge for Montgomery. What a mess, was this evil pervert to affect the lives of more innocent people! I felt a rage fill me up until I thought I was going to choke.

Dead, Ricky was dead, and he had cheated the victim. A nice quick death, one that he hardly felt. I had wanted him to suffer, not die quickly. I wanted him skinned alive, burned at the stake, and gang-raped in prison. I wanted every evil thing I could think of done to him, but I did not want him dead in an instance. How dare he have a relatively painless death! Even the thoughts of him rotting in hell did not please me. I wanted him on a spit roasting slowly while legions of demons stabbed at his flesh with their spears.

Montgomery took me to see a hysterical Tom, who had had to be sedated. I tried to console Tom, but there was no talking to him, so I tried another tactic. I told him I would take him to see his mum, but he refused, and I in my naivety thought it because he was frightened to see her, but oh no, he didn't want to see her. It took a while for me to register that Tom blamed his mum for everything, and I saw red. I shouted at this stupid boy, and I told him of some of the things that Ricky had done to his mum. Things that it wasn't my place to talk about, but I saw them as things that should have had him running to comfort his mum. Tom flinched, but he was unmoved, and he told me that we had planned all along to kill Ricky. He knew Ricky and he knew Ricky could not hurt anyone. We, the police, wanted him as a scapegoat because we could not find the real person who had taken his mum.

I guessed Ricky had fed Tom this garbage on the journey to the station earlier, but I lost my temper with Tom and shook him, screaming that he would soon change his mind when he saw the state of his mum, and I asked where his love for his mum was. I knew I would do Tom serious harm when he screamed back at me, 'My mum brought this on herself. She asked for it,' and then he calmly asked me, did I not understand that he loved Ricky much more than he had ever loved his mum?

Rage like I've never felt before rose in me, and I left Tom in his cell and ran to the morgue. I demanded to see Ricky's stinking body, and when I saw the evil son of a bitch and the peaceful look on his disgusting face, I lost it. I reached for my gun, and I shot his corpse through the head over and over until my gun was empty. All hell broke loose, and Montgomery appeared, grabbed me, and with a few other cops I was disarmed, dragged out, and thrown in a cell.

When Montgomery thought I had calmed down, he opened my cell door, and he told me to go and sit with Rina and when she woke up, I was to get her statement. I told him in no uncertain terms that there would be no statement coming. Ricky was dead, so the police did not need to drag Rina through her nightmare again by reliving it. I told Montgomery that he should get DNA samples from Ricky because I knew that Rina would not be the only woman he had harmed. I handed a subdued and worried Montgomery my badge, and he accepted it. I think he knew my police days were over. Sadly, I walked out of my station for the last time. I did not deserve to wear a police badge. Two strikes, and I was out.

CHAPTER 9

I was to blame we all were. Guardians of the community? I don't think so. We had let Rina down. If she had been a child, we would have searched every house in the street, and the dogs would have found her in minutes. We assumed because there was no evidence that she had just left to start a new life, so this poor woman was handed to her tormentor on a plate. I knew I would carry this guilt around with me until I died, and I swore I would do all I could to help Rina come to terms with her torture and incarceration. I had never been charged, not in a court of law. A jury would find me innocent, but in my conscience, I was guilty, guilty as hell, and the conscience is incapable of deceit, because as this was my second offence, I had no excuse.

I phoned the police station every hour to see if the family knew they were permitted to see Rina. In the end, they would not take my calls. Eventually the husband and I could not believe my eyes, the girlfriend arrived. She knew by my face that she wasn't getting anywhere near Rina, but she told me she was there to support Steve. She would be getting the support of my toe if she was not careful. I was just in time to see the look of disgust flit across Steve's face before he put on an act of sorrow. Crocodile tears trickled, but he knew he wasn't fooling me. I knew he would not be back, so all my hopes were pinned on the daughter, who eventually arrived at midnight dressed like a princess, clutching at the arm of an arrogant-looking man.

At least, Lucy's tears were real, but oh, Rina, what a sorry family you have. Your son-in-law informed me that Lucy had just found out that she was pregnant and he thought it unwise to subject her to this ordeal again. I discovered the real reason later when I saw his picture in the local paper. He was dabbling in politics and did not want himself or Lucy connected to Rina's story. Rina, you are on your own.

I could not stay away from the hospital, so I gave in and decided that I would help the nursing staff with Rina. Was this to be my atonement? I hoped so. I prayed Rina would be my salvation, redemption from my sins. I learned how to massage her limbs to keep them supple, and I learned how to turn her in bed to prevent bed sores, and when I had no nursing duties, I read to her. All this was no burden for it granted me exhaustion, a state I craved, for only exhausted could I sleep in peace.

RINA

CHAPTER 1

I finally asked where my family were, and I knew by the way he blustered and stammered that they were not coming to see me, so I did not ask again. I waited until he went home, and then I let go of my emotions and I cried for the life I had lost. Bitter tears soaked my pillows, but I hardened my heart, and I worked through the pain of my injuries to build up my health. When I was strong and well, I would visit my family, and I would make things right again. I could and would make them see that underneath the marks, I was still me, I was still the same person, I was a wife, a mother, and the person who loved them most in the world, I was only slightly changed by my ordeal, and only on the surface. I would make them see that I was still the same Rina. Deep down, I knew I wasn't, but I would try with every fibre of my being to be normal for them.

I was horrified to find out how long I had been hidden. I know while I was held in that room, it felt like centuries, but at the same time, it passed in a day. I devoured all the back newspapers that Mike could get me, and I welcomed myself back to the world. I had survived, and now, my goal was to get my family back.

Mike would not talk about my abductor except to tell me he was dead, so I decided that I had given Ricky enough of my life and I would banish him from my memory. Mike bought me a plaque that said *I will fear no evil*, and he told me that one day he would explain it to me. He thinks I can't remember anything about my experience, but he is mistaken. I can remember nearly everything. I chose not to think about it.

My treatment, well, I will not pretend, it was anything but hard going, but the thought of my family kept me at it. I had casts on my legs, arms, hands, feet, and for a while on my body itself. The doctors had to break my legs and arms to realign them properly. The pain, oh the pain, but this pain was to restore me to health, to undo what my monster had done to me. The body cast was in case my spine was damaged.

All the physical damage, these wonderful doctors and nurses would cure, but would they be able to cure my damaged mind. Thankfully, I now could use the toilet without the pain making me scream, and best of all, they were able to save my nipple and sew it back on to my breast. At least, my breasts looked normal, well, except for the bite marks.

I talked with myself. I reasoned that I had come through the valley of death itself, so what was a little pain. The rain would soon be gone, and the sun would break through. I was rescued, given another chance, I had something to live for, and I was determined to succeed. The day I walked a few painful steps unaided had everyone in tears. I came on in leaps and bounds. I was still in a lot of pain, but with the help of painkillers, I could live with it, but my face was depressing me. There was only so much the doctors could do. They had fixed my bones, re-plumbed my bodily functions, removed the rest of my rotten teeth, and gave me a sparkly new set, one screwed in, thankfully. My hair had grown thick again, and the hospital hairdresser had dyed it a youthful-looking blonde; even my fingernails and toenails were back and painted a bright shade of red. I had put on some weight, and I looked really good, but I knew I would always carry about with me the reminder of Ricky's abuse.

Mike, dear Mike, he found me in floods of self-pitying tears one day. Did he chide me for being vain? No, he arrived the next day with makeup, and between tears and laughter, I had a makeover and the result pleased me for I felt I could face the world again. I really meant my family.

Chapter 2

I was on a high the day I left hospital although I was sad and a bit apprehensive at leaving this place, which had been a safe and lifesaving haven for me for such a long time, and as I listened to the well wishes of the doctors and nurses who had unstintingly cared for me and had become friends so dear to my heart, I knew I had to make something of the life I had left to me, to thank these wonderful, caring people. I owed my life to their care.

I gathered up my cards, cards sent from the nurses to make up for the lack of family cards, plants bought for me by the same nurses. One day, I vowed, I would make them proud of the woman they had remade and put back together. I was a testament to their skills and compassion, their dedication and care. How could I not regain my life, I had regained my health.

Mike took me home to my new house, a small but pretty bungalow near the sea. I knew he thought the sea air would improve my skin and bring colour to my cheeks. I owed this kind man so much. I hoped one day to pay him back for his loyalty and generosity. I never questioned his reasons for the care he bestowed on me, I never questioned him about anything, I was just so glad to have him first save me, second, look after me. I might have been frightened of any answers that he gave me, and I needed him until I could get my family back. I loved my house, and I felt safe and secure there much to my delight for I had been frightened to leave the hospital where I had been so well-loved and cared for but it was not my home. I did not tell Mike about my thoughts because I sensed he did not share my hopes about my family, and I wondered what had happened between my family and Mike to bring the dark scowl to Mike's face when I mentioned them.

I settled really well into my new house. I really liked everything about it. Mike had guessed me well! I slept soundly, and I woke with a joy in my heart. How I loved to pull back the curtains each morning and see the sea and welcome a bright new day, a day I was alive.

Tom will love my new house, and we can keep it for holidays. I reasoned to myself for I knew foreign holidays were a thing of the past for me. I could not or would not wear revealing summer clothes again. Everything was going to turn out well, I felt it in my bones. I went to the beauty parlour. After her initial shock when she first glimpsed my face, the beauty consultant rose to the challenge, and she taught me how to cover the unsightly marks of Ricky's abuse. I loved her for not asking questions, and I loved her more for the tears that she fought hard to stop welling up in her eyes as she gently smoothed the covering makeup on to my skin. I left her salon a prettier and more confident woman, with a good hair cut, new nails painted bright red. All I needed to complete my armour was new clothes.

Power clothes and even though I was wary of the lingerie dept, I forced myself to buy sexy underwear, now I was ready to do battle. Who had filled my wardrobe with clothes? I had not given this a thought. Had Mike gone to my home and asked for my clothes and been refused? Well, my new clothes made me feel good, more like the Rina of old. I should have worn my track suit, for all the good they did me!

CHAPTER 3

Mike had to go on a trip, and he refused to tell me anything about it, so I guessed this trip had something to do with the demons Mike fought everyday. Mike was a damaged man, it takes one to know one. I hoped one day he would confide in me and let me help him as he had helped me. We were two emotionally disabled people, but we were friends. I knew he was a bit suspicious of my new makeup and hairdo, but he was in a funny subdued mood, so I was able to keep my excitement dampened, hidden, until he left for his trip.

I had planned it well, and Steve and Lucy were at home, but sadly so were Susan and Lucy's husband. My feelings were all over the place when the taxi I had hired slowly moved up my street and my home came into view, my beloved home which brought a huge choking lump to my throat and hot stinging tears to my hungry eyes. My home, my home, at long last, I'm finally home.

Nothing seemed to have changed in my garden, at least nothing I noticed. My shrubs and flowers seemed well cared for and healthy, and I thought this a good omen. My apple tree brought a shiver to my body, an icy shiver, as I remembered the lights that had shone from it on Christmas day. Lights that burnt my eyes as hot as the Christmas lights that *he* had draped around me and burnt my flesh.

Would I be able to eradicate Ricky and his abuse from my mind? Would I actually be able to live here? Yes! This was my home, and I was back to reclaim it. I was back, Rina, wife, mother, and woman. I had dressed with consummate care, and my makeup did what it said on the package, but I knew my face was far from flawless. My new teeth changed the shape of my face, but I did not know if the change was good or bad. I was still their wife and mother. They would want me back when they saw how much I had improved from the wreck of a woman they had visited in the hospital, their one and only visit, but I have to forgive them that. I wondered if guilt had kept them from me, and I meant to assure them that I did not in any way hold them to blame for me not being found for nearly two years. They were my beloved family, and I wanted them back, I wanted my life back, I wanted my home back. I wanted to be Rina again.

CHAPTER 4

I did my best to avoid looking at the house next door, and I rang the bell. Lucy, how beautiful you are and I am over the moon to discover I am to be a grandmother and quite soon by the size of you. I hugged you or tried to, but you were so stiff and unresponsive in my arms that I dropped them and pushed past you on into the house. There she is, my nemesis. A white hot anger flowed in my veins, and I imagined it was visible because they all paled as they stared open-mouthed at me. Steve was the first to recover and jumped up and shook my hand. Shook my hand, this is my husband, the man whom I have slept with, and was as intimate as any person can be with another, he is shaking my hand.

It is then I notice that Lucy is not the only pregnant lady in the family. I look around my home or what was once my home, and the reality hits me hard so hard that even though I can see their mouths open and close, I can't hear what they are saying for the roaring in my ears—the roaring of rage, hopelessness, and overwhelming despair.

Susan has won, and I am not to have the revenge I so desired and planned for. What did I really think Steve would do when he saw me? Was I so deluded to imagine he would want me, a damaged and polluted woman over and above this pretty young woman sitting so smugly at his side? Did I really think that because I was the mother of his children, he would see sense and put our torn family back together again? He had discarded me and oh so easily replaced me. I had nothing to fight with, but she had fought and planned the battle well and I could only retreat in the face of her overwhelming success. How could I compete with a child, especially when, thanks to my abductor, I was physically incapable of carrying any more babies. The age-old difference it seemed, from being a wanted woman and an unwanted one, barrenness. Susan seems to swell and grow in my vision, and I begin to shrivel and fade in the beam of her success. I am destroyed.

I refuse to let them see me cry, so I make my way to Tom's room, thinking I will find him there. Tears blinding me, I realise Tom's room is changed and I am in their bedroom, Steve and Susan's. I want to tear it apart. I look at their bed, and I am enraged to find it is our bed, the bed where I loved my husband. the bed where I sat in the early hours and fed my babies. How could he. Had he no decency, no heart. I need to sit down, but I do not want to sit on this bed because I imagine I can see the pair of them naked, entwined together, and I am choking on my hatred of them.

I stumble to the room that used to be my bedroom, mine and Steve's, and Steve appears with a key and hands it to me before disappearing. He is a coward. He knew what I would see, but he left me on my own to view the pictures of Tom and myself stuck all over the walls. Was my husband always this weak? When had he become this cold, cruel, and thoughtless man? I studied him as he walked away from me, back to Susan, and one word came to my mind—dreary. When did Steve become dreary?

Our family pictures, photos that I had looked forward to seeing again but not now, now they told me just what my son thought of me and I knew I might never see my son again. In every picture, my face was scratched and scored, and beside Tom in most of the photos was a cut-out of Ricky's face. At that moment, I wished Ricky had killed me and spared me from ever seeing this ultimate betrayal.

How long I sat there on Tom's bed with my head in my hands I don't know, but the taxi driver ringing on the doorbell forced me back from my despair. His anxious inquiry for me was soft balm to my heart, and it gave me the courage and determination to move.

I decided to remove all the pictures and to throw out all of my clothes that seemed to be everywhere in this room. I went into the kitchen, and I discovered the black bin bags in the same place they always were, and I returned to Tom's room, and I filled all the bags with anything that had ever belonged to me. My family clearly did not want me, so I was determined to wipe out all traces of myself from their midst.

I discovered bottles and bottles of the perfume I used to like, and they were nearly my undoing because I realised that until Ricky had poisoned Tom against me, my son must have missed me dreadfully. I took one last look around to implant some resemblance of my son in my mind, and then I opened the wardrobe. There hanging on an ordinary wooden coat hanger was my jogging outfit, and as I lifted it out, a memory flooded back so strongly that I cried out and collapsed on to the bed. I remember I was wearing this the night I had been snatched. I was going to go for a run after I had put the milk bottles out, but I tripped over the cat, and then I noticed how glorious the stars were and I never got to run. The rest as they say is history. I hold my outfit against my face, and I detect a faint smell of lavender, so my abductor had had the audacity to put the clothes I had worn the night he had snatched me back in among my other clothes and no one had noticed!

My tears stopped. This was not my home any more. I have been replaced by a new younger, fertile model. My heart felt like lead as I acknowledged that I was on my own, no husband, no son, and now no daughter. Is this how an innocent man feels when he is jailed for something that he did not do. The self-pity was choking me. I had planned for my family welcoming me home. I had planned for wreaking revenge on Susan. Yes, I was realistic in knowing I had bridges to mend, especially in regard to Tom. I had even planned how I would deal with intimacy with Steve, but at no time had I planned for my unmitigated defeat at their hands. I would never see inside my home again; a home is made up of the people inside it, and this home did not want me. Leaving my home this time was worse than the last time, when Ricky took me. He had dragged me away; now, I had to drag myself away for ever.

The taxi driver helped me load the black bags into his cab and thankfully said nothing. In his line of work, he has probably seen it all. I went back to face my family, and I told Steve I wanted my half of what the house was worth, and I turned to my daughter, but words failed me, so I walked out the front door of my home or rather the house I used to live in for the last time. I searched the garden for my cat, but I could not find her, and as I stood in the side garden, I forced myself to look up at the window where I had spent most of my days in captivity.

I stared at an ordinary window dressed up in very pretty pink gingham with a *My Little Pony* on the window ledge, and I guessed a little girl slept there now. I prayed she would fill the sad room with laughter and happiness and banish my tears and heartbreak. I hoped the new neighbours would chase the ghosts of my terrors away and make this a loving home full of normal loving people.

I instructed the driver to go to the dump, and he kindly helped me dispose of my past and then he drove me home to my new life, a new life I planned to live to the full. The plans of mice and men, I wish I could remember it, something about going astray.

STEVE

CHAPTER 1

I remember the day we realised Rina was missing. I harboured a faint hope that she had found out about Susan and had decided to walk, but it was not really Rina's style to walk away from trouble. When had I stopped loving her? The day I realised Rina was a strong woman. I hated the way she argued and debated with me. I found her aggressive and manly. I believed I had married a quiet young girl whom I could mould and groom to my liking, but I had married a woman with strengths and a determination to do things her way. I hated the way she voiced her opinions in front of our friends. In fact, the more our friends admired her, the more I disliked her.

I constantly felt in competition with her over every aspect of our lives, and I was sick of the way she made me feel inadequate. Even in bed, I did not appreciate her wantonness. She seemed to revel in pleasure. I found it unbecoming in a wife. She acted in bed like the prostitutes my friends and I enjoyed on our work trips. I certainly did not want this in a wife. When she started to help out at the crisis centre, the writing was on the wall for our marriage. I had put up with her helping all and sundry with their problems, but this was a step too far. Where was she when I needed her? I liked a properly run home, granted she worked hard to keep it in order, but I wanted a wife, not a woman who was out at all hours either fixing people's ruined marriages or lives, when her own marriage was disintegrating.

Did she notice? I don't think so. Rina lived a life believing everyone thought as she did. I started to hate her so got my own back for her neglect of me by screwing as many of Rina's friends as I could get to drop their pants. She did neglect me, my own mother agreed with me. I came at the bottom of her list after the children, cat, neighbours, and her mental friends at the crisis centre. How could she not have known what I was about or maybe she did know and she didn't care, but when I met Susan, I discovered the soft, pliable, homely woman I should have married.

Chapter 2

I was planning on telling Rina about Susan when she disappeared, so I am not surprised that the policemen thought I was a bit off when they questioned me about her whereabouts. How could I explain to them that I never knew where my wife was from one second to the next with her work at the centre and her jogging at all hours of the night. Let them try to live with a woman who lives her life the way she wants regardless of what her husband desires. Their faces when I told them about Susan nearly made me laugh, but I was soon filled with disgust and fear when I realised they suspected me of killing her.

I knew I did not touch her, and soon, well not as soon as I would have liked, they stopped their questions, and they accepted that Rina had discovered all about Susan and had buggered off, and because there is no evidence to show an abduction, they have finally left us alone.

Tom is all over the place about Rina, and he is doing my head in with his dramas. Rina is gone about six months now, and the police have stepped down their enquiries, well, all but one of them. A big guy called Mike something. I hate the way he turns up out of the blue to check up on us. I have complained about him, but he still calls every now and then hoping to catch us out some way. He is wasting his time. Whatever happened to Rina had nothing to do with any of us. I do hope she is well. I would not like to think of her hurt, but I am happy that her disappearance has enabled me to live the life I deserve. I don't miss her, but the house does, and I can't wait until I can move Susan in as my wife. I can't marry her until Rina's disappearance is explained, but to have her here beside me every day is something I yearn for. Tom is the thorn in my flesh, but Lucy is remarkable. She has fallen head over heels in love with a guy very much like myself, and he has helped her to come to terms with her mother's disappearance. Lucy stays in his family home most of the time now, and if it wasn't for Tom, I would be a happy man for the first time in years. Thank goodness for Ricky, our funny little new neighbour; he is a bit old for Tom to be fooling around with, but he keeps Tom out of my hair, so I am happy to welcome him at any time. He has been so thoughtful and generous to us as a family, and Rina would have loved him.

I had a tear in my eye for Rina when Lucy got married, but Susan was delightful, and the day went smoothly except for that stupid, arrogant policeman who had the cheek to attend.

So here we are a happy family, and Rina is found and things are never the same again.

CHAPTER 3

I will never forget the sight of her. She should have died. I don't mean
that in a bad way. I just think it would have been better for her and
everyone else if Rina had died. I am just being honest and saying out
loud what I believe everyone else is thinking. She was like an animal
that had been caught in a trap for weeks. And the stink of her was
so bad I had to run to the bathroom to vomit. I thought my stomach
was never going to settle. It took me ages to forget that smell, and I
refused to go back to that place. I had nightmares, just thinking about
her ordeal, and I took panic attacks every time the police called to ask
us to visit. Susan understood and convinced me it was not in my best
interests or good for my health to visit Rina. Did we abandon her? I
don't think so. She in her decision to put herself in danger destroyed
her family. I'm not for one moment suggesting it was her own fault,
but everyone has a responsibility to avoid putting themselves and their
family in the way of danger.

I have a new family now, and Lucy has a new family. We have
moved on, and now that Rina is safe and well, she can move on with
her life also. Tom was the only fly in the ointment, but I am convinced
he will calm down, and if I am honest, I really don't need him here with
the new baby coming and all. I hope he does not return but makes a
new life for himself. Who would have thought the bold Ricky so evil
and cunning. How mistaken I was. I actually miss him and his lovely
food he used to bring over for us. I can't believe the things the police

told me he had done to those young girls, and I wonder if Tom is right and the police are using him as a scapegoat. Strange things can happen in police stations.

What a nightmare when Rina just appeared at the front door, and I thought she would never have the courage to come back to her house after what had happened to her on that same doorstep. None of us could speak, we were so shocked; Susan dear love her, her face was white as a sheet and it's no wonder the venomous look Rina directed at her. I did not know what to do for the best when she said she was going to Tom's room. I could hardly stop her, stop Rina. A rhino could not have stopped Rina. I had to explain that we had swapped rooms, and I gave her the key to Tom's room, but I had forgotten all about the pictures. I had meant to remove them, but as I never for one moment thought Rina would be back, let alone see them, I was in no hurry. We all heard her cries, and we did feel bad for her, but what can anyone do, her life here is no more, and we are helpless to comfort her. Lucy just hides her face in her husband's coat, and he frowns more than usual. He is a man of little words, especially about Rina. I imagine he pretends she does not exist, and one day, he will probably wipe her from Lucy's mind altogether.

Thankfully, the taxi driver knocks on the door, and as we are all rooted to the spot and can't move, Rina answers the door and instructs the driver that she will need help with her bags. I hear her rummaging in the cupboard under the sink, and I am too confused to move, so the four of us sit silently where we are and wait until she comes for us. I don't recognise the woman I married in this termagant that stands in front of me and demands that I give her half of what my house is worth. How dare this woman who has destroyed this family now try to wreak havoc on my new family. I did try to remonstrate with her, but I made a mistake mentioning the baby. No amount of makeup or expensive new teeth can cover up what Ricky did to her. She is an ugly woman, and anger makes the marks on her face stand out more vividly. Lucy refuses to come out from her husband's coat, so Rina finally, and not before time, leaves us, and I hope, for the last time. I do feel for her, but life is tough and we have to move on or sink in the mire.

LUCY

CHAPTER 1

Mummy, Mummy, please forgive me, Mum. I can't deal with seeing you with his marks all over you. It made me sick just to think of you and what he did to you. How could you stand it? I would have died in your place if he had done those things to me. I'm sure there are days that you wished you had died when you have to face going out in public looking as you do.

That policeman was so wrong to tell us just about everything that you had gone through. I think he delighted in the gory details. We did not need to know the details. In fact, Mark has put a complaint in against him. Mark told him that I was upset, but he just said I should be. What does it have to do with him anyway? He is not family, but you would think he was by the way he acted in the hospital. He made me feel bad, and I really, really missed you when you went, and I even missed you telling me what I should or should not do. I always thought I would enjoy a life doing whatever I wanted, but I was floundering without you to keep me right until Mark came into my life. I love him so very much, and he is everything I ever wanted. He helped me come to terms with your disappearance, but like us all, he thought you had left because of Susan. If I had thought of you in pain, I would have died, but I thought of you somewhere safe with another man. I did not blame you. I would have done the same if I had been married to Dad. He was impossible before Susan moved in. He expected me, me to do all the work.

Tom was a nightmare until he fell in love with Ricky, but he is wrong if he thinks Ricky was gay. Ricky tried to sleep with me the night before my wedding, so he is definitely not gay.

Mark carried my burden for me and rescued me from madness, and now we are married and having our first child, he likes me to stay calm and not get overwrought. I used to cry all the time when you left. The house was a real mess, only for Ricky bringing us food, which was delicious, we would have starved.

Mark and his parents are my world, and I feel so safe and secure with them. They are so accomplished and so rich. Mark's mum did not like Susan. I'm sure you are glad to hear. She does not like Daddy much either, and I know if things had been different, you and she would get along well. I wish you could see their house. It is enormous. They have bought us a lovely house as well as paying for a six-month honeymoon, just to help us get away from it all. We stayed in Hawaii, and you should have seen all the beautiful gifts that I brought everyone home. If I had known I would see you again, I would have bought you something special.

My house is lovely, six bedrooms, and Marcie, my mother-in-law, who makes me call her mumsie, LOL, has helped me to decorate it beautifully. We have five bedrooms and a special nursery full of everything a baby could want, more than Susan's baby will have, LOL.

I will let you know when our baby is born, and you can come and stay. Oh sorry, have to go, Mark is home, must show him my letter.

CHAPTER 2

I'm sorry, Mummy, but Mark feels I should concentrate on the baby and let you settle into your new life and maybe some day in the future we will visit with our child. Now that we have moved house, Mark thinks it a good idea not to give our new address out to my family. It is a pity you can't see my new home. It is so beautiful. Mark has denied me nothing; he has surrounded me with wonderful things; and I am blissfully happy, not that I was so unhappy before, well before you went but now well, I am treated like a princess. I am happy to do anything he asks, not that he asks me to do anything I don't want to do.

It does sadden me a little when I think back to the happy times we had once, but as Mark says, we are building a new family, and we want our child born into happiness and beauty. I missed you on my wedding day, but Susan was great and soon had me beaming like a bride. She went to so much trouble, and Ricky, well, what would we have done without Ricky and yet the police say he took you. It is all so unbelievable; he was so kind to us when you were away.

I do love you, Mum, but I love Mark more, and I want to be surrounded by serenity and peace now that I am to become a mother myself. I'm sure you understand. Mark says you do, and I know you want the best for me as I wish for you. Hopefully, one day when we have all settled down and are secure in our lives, we will meet again. Hopefully, you will heal and be the pretty Rina once more.

CHAPTER 3

I read the letter I wrote to my mum just before I posted it, but I did not send it. Don't ask me why because I really don't know. I play a game now as I wait for the birth of my first child. I pretend I am adopted, and I don't know who my parents are.

MIKE

CHAPTER 1

I was really looking forward to seeing Rina and the progress she has made. I had left her buoyant and happy but the sight that met me as she opened her door, after I had threatened to break it down because she had refused to answer it or me and I knew she was inside. She had lost the sparkle she had gained in the hospital, and instead, the lost look was back in her eyes. Gone was the new makeup, and the bite marks stood out clearly on the dry undernourished skin. She was a mess and had not washed or brushed her hair, and I was shocked to see her in the state she was in. This was so unlike the Rina I had come to love and cherish. I was horrified and demanded to know what had happened.

I realised I should not have left her, but I made my pilgrimage every year and to miss it would kill me. I tried to talk to her, but she just shrugged her shoulders and said what did it matter she might as well be dead for what good was she to anyone and no one wanted her. She went on and on about how hard she had tried to overcome her trials but she could not find anything to live for. When she started crying, 'Why me, why me, what did I ever do to deserve this? My life is over. He might as well have killed me for I am useless now,' my patience with this woman evaporated, and I grabbed her arm and dragged her out to my car. I was incensed, and I knew I was hurting her, but this was worth a gamble, and I had to try one last time and then I would leave her on her own. I could do no more, I was exhausted, and I had my own demons to fight. I acknowledged and realised that I had not Montgomery's perseverance or his good heart.

CHAPTER 2

We drove in complete silence, my body rigid with annoyance, hers with ill-concealed fury until we turned into the drive of *Sunshine House*, and once, again my spirits lifted as they always did at the sight of this grand old house standing like a castle at the end of a flower-filled drive. I stopped the car, and Rina jumped out before I had the chance to grab her again. *We* walked, not speaking, into the large welcoming house, into the sound of laughter and chatter.

We walked in and out of each bright and shiny room in this house of suffering, and we smiled at every child and parent in them. I spoke to the ones I knew, and I introduced Rina, but she never spoke one word. She couldn't for I knew she was frightened to open her mouth. I knew the emotions she was working hard to suppress. Rina did well until we were driving out of the gate when she slapped me so hard across the face I had to fight to keep control of the car and then the tears came, fast and furious, but they were not tears of self-pity, they were tears of shame. I drove Rina home, and over coffee, I told Rina where I had been and the reason why I had cared for her in the hospital.

CHAPTER 3

I told her about my lovely young wife, Carrie, and my beautiful little boy, Adam, and how I had killed them. I began at the beginning of my happy life when I met a beautiful young woman called Carrie, a girl out of my league, born into a wealthy family, but she fell in love with me, me, a mere rookie cop, and my life changed forever. How I loved her and how happy we were until one day just before our wedding, I overheard her parents talking and I heard her father ask if Carrie was doing the right thing in marrying well below her station in life, would she not miss all the extras that came with having money. I heard this, and a seed of determination germinated in my heart. I chose to remember her father's question, but I also chose to ignore her mother's answer, that Carrie loved me for who I was and not what I had and that Carrie was a lovely girl not impressed by wealth. I should have cultivated her mother's love and not her father's doubts.

I loved my job as a policeman, loved it so much that I was on call every second of the day. My wife accused me of loving my job more than I loved her, but I was trying to prove to myself and to others that I was material for chief inspector, one day in the future. I worked all the hours God sent, and I neglected my wee family in the journey to be the best cop.

When did the unhappiness creep in — Carrie's because she thought I neglected her, mine when I failed to make her understand that I was doing this for her. I was annoyed with her because why could she not understand and cut me some slack. A few years and I could slow down, but I had to work hard or others would snatch what I so desperately craved. I needed to show Carrie's dad that I could give her more than he had. I was as good as him. I was successful. What I did not see or realise was that Carrie loved me and hated my job.

Our peaceful happy life had all but evaporated when Carrie found out she was pregnant, and I was overjoyed. I cut back on my workload, and I spent time with my lovely wee wife and we fell in love all over again. What a happy, happy time in my life and the memories and lack of them shatter my heart into thousands of pieces. I can never explain the joy in my heart when I held my little son, Adam, in my arms. We were complete, and I was the happiest man in the world. We were very happy, but once again I let a remark of Carrie's dad destroy my family. No, I cannot blame him for he meant no harm, but the seed was once more planted in my heart, and I watered it well. It grew to be a bigger monster than the first one.

Once again, I needed to prove myself, especially now with a child to support; my son would go to the best schools, no primary for him, he would go to prep just like his mum. How Carrie pleaded with me and begged me to spend more time with her and Adam, but she made me irate by not understanding that I needed a few years to make a proper and good life for us.

I worked all the hours I could again, and I tried so hard to show my wife and son my love when I had time with them, but invariably our time together was awkward and unrewarding because I was tired all the time and Carrie was simmering with resentment towards me. Why, oh why did I not spend more time at home and enjoy my wee family when I had them and now it is too late for me. I remember that awful night as if it were yesterday, that terrible night when my life came crashing down around me, the night I killed my most precious possessions.

CHAPTER 4

I had as usual come home late exhausted from working a straight twenty hours, and Carrie had left me a curt note that said my dinner was in the bin, to help myself, this made me laugh, but I was glad she wrote not to waken her or Adam. Why, oh why did I not just ignore her note and race up the stairs, pick my little son up, and drink him in. Why, oh why did I not shower and snuggle up in bed with my beautiful young wife. I can't even remember the last time we made love, and this thought tortures the life out of me as I try to visualise her lying in my arms softly gazing up at me as I make love to her. No, I can only visualise her sad and angry face as she pleads with me to spend more time at home, more time that I would give the world for now.

Stupid man. I decided I was hungry so I thought I'd make myself some chips. Why did I not send for a takeaway, why did I not just make a sandwich or grab some crisps. No, I decided to make big fat chips. I put fat in the pan, and I sat down to listen to some music but I was exhausted and I soon fell asleep. The phone ringing woke me. I belligerently answered a call from my station informing me about a man seen in the high street brandishing a gun and would I follow it up. They knew I would, they knew I never turned away anything that would help make my name as the best cop in the force. I shook myself awake, grabbed my jacket, and ran out my front door. I had not even checked on my wife and child because I did not want any grief from Carrie about the ruined dinner. I reckoned if she woke, she would know I was working and she would be so mad. Now I know just how sad, not mad my Carrie was.

The hot fat bubbled and bubbled, it grew and grew, soon it would change colour, it would be black. Dark, smoky black, and then the first flicker of flame would ignite a torrent of red orange and gold. I prayed that the smoke had really killed them long before the hot scorching flames found them. I raced to rescue an unknown stranger who meant nothing to me. How honourable, how great of me, and I left my wife and child, whom I had promised to love and protect, to burn to death, without hope of rescue from anyone.

CHAPTER 5

How kind and generous people can be, even when they do not mean it. They told me I was not to blame and I should not feel guilty. It was one of those things that could happen to anyone, any one of us. No, no, no, it could not happen to anyone. It could only happen to someone who lived a life of altruism. Oh, I knew I was to blame. The fault lay entirely at my feet. I had promised to love honour and care for my wife. I had promised my son that I would always be there for him. The day he was born I promised him that I would do all in my power to protect him from evil and harm that dwelt in this world.

Words, words, words, uttered but not absorbed. His wonderful protector led him to his destruction, and I would never forgive the role I played in his and his mother's death. There was absolutely nothing any one of my good friends could do that would assuage the guilt that I lived with each day. More platitudes that life would go on, the pain would lessen each day and the old favourite that time heals. I did not want any lessening of my hurt. I eagerly accepted the guilt because I deserved it and more. I should have been the one that died, and if I could, I would gladly change places with my two precious ones. My punishment was waking up each day and reliving the horror that I had unleashed on my family. I would never complain about my punishment. It did not in any stretch of the imagination fit my crime.

Everyone was so very understanding and said it was an accident and that Carrie and Adam were dead before the fire reached them, but

I know it wasn't a accident. I did not do it on purpose, but nevertheless, I killed them, and every night before I fall asleep, I see them, Carrie cuddling Adam in her arms as the dark swirling, choking smoke slowly takes their life away. I should have been done for murder for I know I killed them.

So, Rina, you see I am a monster too, but I had a friend who rescued me from my nightmare, a very good man who stopped me taking the easy way out. Montgomery helped me in my darkest hour and stopped me spiralling out of control and hurting any one else. He cared enough to help me want to live. He persevered and dragged me out of the pit of despair, and so I am passing it on, and I am trying to help you face your demons so that you too can live.

We have to live. Life is so fragile but also such a gift. It is not to be thrown away when so many have their lives snatched away. Even if we are not worth living for ourselves, we are worth living for others. I volunteer in *Sunshine House* because I want to show Montgomery that saving me was worth his while. I told Rina of my visits home once a year, to put flowers on and to sit by my wife and son's grave and to tell them I am sorry and that I will love them until I die. I don't ask for forgiveness; there is none for my crime. I was crying as I left Rina. I was exhausted, heart sore, and felt I had no more to give. I was an empty shell; it was up to her now. She had to want to live. I could show her the flowers, but I could not make her smell their fragrance, see their beauty, and gather them up in her arms, and make a glorious bouquet. That is what life is all about, bouquets of flowers.

RINA

CHAPTER 1

Poor, poor Mike, his story touched me when nothing else had. I had been so selfish. I realised I had fallen into the 'why me, what have I ever done to deserve this' brigade. Yes, I had come through a terrible ordeal, yes I was scarred inside and out, yes I was frightened almost every second of the day, yes I had lost my family, and they had replaced me with others, but I lived, I lived and I could go on, deep down I knew I could, but only I and I alone could achieve this. In place of the huge tumour of fear that Ricky had planted, which I now uprooted, I planted a tiny, very, very tiny seed, so tiny that I would have to be protective of it, but in my heart, I knew this seed would grow and grow and I could hardly wait to see what it produced. I hoped it would grow into a gorgeous flower, but I would gladly settle for a buttercup.

So I dusted myself down, and I spring-cleaned my home until it squeaked. The next day, as fair as I could make myself with makeup and nice clothes, saw me, at the door of *Sunshine House*, if they wanted me, I desperately wanted them. I had been volunteering there for about a week when I bumped into Mike, and I laughed to see the amazed look on his face when he realised it really was me. He picked me up in his strong arms, and to the delight of the kids and their parents, he swung me round until I squealed for him to stop. How delighted the children were to see me dizzy and trying my best to walk without falling over. Mike is a true friend indeed.

CHAPTER 2

Sunshine House, well named for it is full of sunshine. It is also full of sorrow and the worse kind of heartache because children come here to die from the cancer that is robbing them of life. I have been taught a huge hard lesson here. Six months have passed for me in a blur of raw emotions, and I am ashamed at how I tried and dismally failed to come to terms with my ordeal. I look at these sick children who are being abducted and tortured by a monster far worse than mine and yet they are courageous and much braver than I ever was. They face their torment every waking moment. At least I was reprieved while my monster slept, but their monster never sleeps but roars like a lion and devours all of their bodies and consumes their minds. Do they bemoan their lot like I did? No, not a bit of it. They live what life they have left to the full, in making poignant memories, beautiful memories for their families that they reluctantly leave behind. I was rescued and my monster slayed, but their monster can only die when they themselves die, so these precious children can't be saved. They have no choice about living, but I do.

Now I no longer ask why me, why not me, for am I more precious than any one of these children. Am I more important than them? I have been given a second chance, more than they have, and I mean to make the most of it. I will prove to Mike that I was worth saving.

I lost my heart to one little boy, Josh, and it wasn't just because he said I was beautiful; it was because I had never seen such courage in adversary as I saw Josh show. I would have gladly given my life for his, but that is not how it works, and I miss him so much.

I think of my own family in times when I have a moment of solitude, but they are soft thoughts of years gone past, and I refuse to dwell on the trauma that Ricky caused. It was hard to come to the realisation that my family did not want me. I went over and over in my mind just how bad to them I must have been for them to reject me. What had I done to them to make them indifferent to me? Thoughts that brought no answers; I would never know why my family were not glad to see me alive. I knew deep down they would have preferred me dead than returning to blight their lives. They had 'moved on', and I had to also.

I have a new family now. The children are my children, and I love them as much as I ever loved my own and my heart breaks as each little one loses their fight and silently slips away. We are left with their photographs and their colourful drawings that decorate our walls. I noticed something about their pictures. There is no black in their drawings; the children use only the brightest colours. The colours of the rainbow, and as I walk about in Sunshine House in the middle of the night, yes, I am still a night person and I gladly stay when I am needed, these rainbow colours shine and glow, and I imagine I see the artists smiling down on me.

I mourn along with their parents; they are my family, and my family grows bigger and bigger every day as I keep in touch with these heartbroken people. People who will in their own time come back and share in the joy of caring for these special children, and like me their hearts will be healed and their lives enriched. I am truly blessed. I wake each day with a song in my heart, and sunshine sparkles in my life and I acknowledge I am happy. I am really happy. In fact, I am happier in my new life than I ever was in my old one, and I thank God each day.

I opened an envelope today, while I ate my breakfast, a plain white, ordinary envelope that had come in the post and had my name printed on the front, with a stamp indicating the letter was from India. Who did I know in India? As I opened it, a photo fell out on to the table. A photograph that had been taken in my old garden, a picture of me swinging a smiling Tom round and round.

The End

Printed in Great Britain
by Amazon

82509608R00109